Henry Cornes was a children's television researcher at the BBC before moving on to lecturing in art and fashion history at various universities and colleges. He lives in London and makes stained glass windows when not writing fashion books.

Henry Cornes

FAST FASHION AND FLANEURS

FFFashion

AUSTIN MACAULEY PUBLISHERS™

LONDON • CAMBRIDGE • NEW YORK • SHARJAH

A CIP catalogue record for this title is available from the British Library.

ISBN 9781528976190 (Paperback)
ISBN 9781528976213 (ePub e-book)

www.austinmacauley.com

First Published (2020)
Austin Macauley Publishers Ltd
25 Canada Square
Canary Wharf
London
E14 5LQ

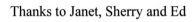
Thanks to Janet, Sherry and Ed

Prologue

'You couldn't buy Marx's coat in one of your fast fashion shops,' were the last words Bill Wonder heard as he fell to his death from the 8th floor balcony of his prestigious London fashion school. He didn't understand the inference then, although he did before he hit the ground. But the words 'fast fashion' had been flung at him like sartorial swear words. He wondered if he should feel guilty for the inexcusable wrong he was now being punished for with his life. The feeling was only fleeting – he mainly felt pride: overwhelming, smug, self-satisfied pride for his achievements in life. He had dictated what the UK should wear for 30 years and his personal worth was just over £8 billion. The only thing that pricked his conscience now was, had he known he was going to die today, he would have worn a tailor-made suit or better still a suit from the men's outfitter shop he had just opened in Regent Street, next to his arch rival NFFW. Not the cheap torn schmutter he was dressed in now.

As Bill's body hit the pavement he muttered, 'Damn that corsetiere, I should never have crossed her.'

The building shook more than it should and an icy scream echoed through the busy shops on Oxford Street. Consumers stopped and looked at each other, aware that something monumental had just happened, something that would change the very fabric of shop-hungry Oxford Street and somehow they knew shopping for clothes would never be the same again.

Chapter 1
One Butt at a Time

I was having a vivid stripy monotone Op art to Mondrian colour block dream about who invented the mini skirt first. The dream was taking place in the shop window of Mary Quant's Bazaar shop on the Kings Road.

Mary was saying, 'I definitely invented it first.'

Then the designer John Bates stuttered in an unsung hero way, 'B-b-but my dresses were shorter and I also like to expose midriff and cleavage and I insist women wear no underwear. Surely that makes me the first.'

As they both stand around breezily not agreeing, Robby the Robot from the film Forbidden Planet crashes into the window holding a dead or swooning Anne Francis. Robby speaks in a punctuated drone, 'The mini skirt was first seen in the 1956 film, Forbidden Planet.'

Then just as Robbie is righting Anne Francis, Bill Wonder's large angry face looms in through a screen print daisy backdrop and shouts, 'How much?'

I wake up with a jolt, my heart pounding; my first thought is, *Oh shit, I'm going to be late for work, what will the Year 1 Fashion Diploma students do without my insightful lecture on 1960s' teen marketing.*

Then a wave of relief embroidered over me as I remembered I didn't need to be at work until 10 o'clock today as the Diploma students were at the World Retail Clothes exhibition at Olympia and I went back to sleep. I had just fallen back into a somnolent multi-coloured beatnik daze and had just started to mull the great mini skirt debate. Why did women in the sixties think that walking around in clothes so short that everyone could see their knickers was somehow a reflection of female emancipation when the landline rang. *No one rings the landline anymore,* I thought, *well apart from Bubbe, possibly the police and telemarketing firms.*

'Hello,' I said with a strange prescience that it wasn't going to be good news.

'Hello Sadie, it's Gita from HR.'

'Gita,' I gasped.

'Sadie I am very sorry to say this but you have been suspended and you can't come into work until we have resolved certain issues.'

'What issues?' I asked then nervously babbled, 'I have finished the wall displays for the open day they're on my desk. I will be there in thirty minutes. Surely Bill can wait that long, can't he.'

'Sadie this has nothing to do with wall displays and as it's 6.45 am you are not late.'

'But why have I been suspended then?' I cried uncomprehendingly.

'Don't press me,' Gita replied.

'Am I pressing you?' I asked even more confused.

'Sadie, we will pay you full pay whilst the incident is being investigated but you must not contact anyone from the office or come in whilst the investigation is ongoing.'

'But I don't know what the incident is,' I cried. 'Should I get my union involved?'

'Sadie, I don't like your tone. Are you threatening the company?' Gita replied, her tone changing from placating to icy in an instant.

'No, I'm trying to understand why I have been suspended,' I pleaded.

'Sadie you mentioned the union, I would like to remind you that we don't recognise the union here.'

'Yes, I know,' I sighed dejectedly. I had seen other staff clear their desks before they had time to clench their fists.

Gita finally seemed to let go of some of her HR veneer and said, (I think honestly) 'I don't know what you have done but you have really annoyed head office. It's probably a mistake and will be sorted out soon. But in the meantime, do not contact anyone from the school.'

'What should I do?' I asked rather pathetically.

Gita sighed and then said in a consolatory way, 'I heard you worked late last night. Have a lie in today. Have a facial, go to the hairdresser's and get your nails done. I will be in touch.'

The phone went dead.

I took a good look at myself in the mirror after Gita's ontological advice and she was right, I did look a bit dull. My hair was a touch too long. My nails were non-existent, my stomach had swelled from one too many salted caramel muffin lunches eaten at my desk and my polyester pretend designer clothes look like the sartorial equivalent of stultiloquence chitchat. I wondered whether Bill had suspended me because I look horrible. I mean I did work at the Bill Wonder's Fashion school the pinnacle of, "nothing tastes as good as skinny feels" educational academies and I had noticed that Bill was very exacting when it came to what people look like. When Alistair came back from the Christmas break looking like his mother had overfed him lard cakes, Bill stopped him and said very loudly, 'Who ate all the pies?' and he had often stopped Mags Twill when she lolloped in and said slightly obtuse things like, 'Maybe your washing machine has broken again.'

Had my tired, knackered outward appearance simply been too much for the school's aesthetics? *Well if that's the case,* I thought whilst humming the theme tune from Rocky I, *I will have to put that right and actually as I've been suspended, I have the time to just do it as well.*

'Now what I need is an empowering new look,' I muttered whilst flicking through Haute the magazine for people with style and vast sums of money. I noted that a fierce Coco Chanel bob was on trend and as Chanel really has to be way up there on the strong independent woman ranking, aside from a few ethical and moral issues. I decided to go for it.

At the hairdressers I said, 'Cut my hair into a blunt bob,' and showed Gulsum the hairdresser a picture of a young Coco.

Gulsum grimaced, 'Are you sure, we will have to cut off all your Ali MacGraw's?'

Four hours later, my hair was a sharp symmetrical line just below my ears.

'You will probably need to sleep in a hair net to keep the shape,' Gulsum said, sounding worried.

I looked at myself; it was hard to say whether it looked nice, I think different came to mind. 'Just one more thing, really your mushy Cara's should go and I suggest a shellac buff.'

I looked confused.

'Your eyebrows need to be plucked and reshaped into a high arch. We're offering a two for one, so you may as well get your nails done as well. Shall I call Robbie?'

I nodded passively.

'So, I hear you're flaunting fashion?' Robbie said whilst brandishing cruel tweezers. 'Leave it to me.'

In between wincing at the plucks and buffs, I fumed about the suspension.

'All done,' said Robbie clasping his hands together in a cutesy way. I fully opened my eyes and really had no idea who the reflection staring back at me was.

On the way home, I stared out of the black on grey tube windows and decided to retrace exactly what had happened the day before. Assuming that my transgression had happened last night as Gita had accidentally let slip; I rewound the chain of events. Tanya the principal was leaning on the door frame of her office looking confused and wanting. She was wearing a Giorgio Armani vertically striped, black and white jacket and skirt and I think bag and shoes. Her flustered zebraic ensemble made my eyes hurt, and I hurried past with my head down praying that the impossible would happen and she somehow wouldn't delineate me in between the black and white lines. My invisibility plan didn't work and she brayed something like, 'Silver, that's your name isn't it, you can organise a few wall displays for the school's open day tomorrow before you go home.'

I had briefly tried to remonstrate but knew full well my fate was sealed.

I remembered feeling like a marked man as I walked into the office. Everyone was busy putting on coats and exchanging niceties.'

Jonathan said, 'Thank god, it's Friday in five days' time.'

Mags Twill replied, 'Yes, I'll drink to that.'

As the room emptied, Josue from facilities arrived with his yellow sack truck stacked high with white storage boxes. 'Delivery for Sadie,' he said in his sunny Mediterranean way.

'There are rather a lot of them,' I replied glumly.

'Si, si, si, there are boxes everywhere, what with the remodelling of Bill's head office and Bill temporarily moving to the third floor, all sorts of boxes everywhere,' Josue replied sagely.

'Ok,' I said, despairingly eyeing the first two boxes.

'Sadie, will you be working late tonight?' Josue asked sweetly.

'Late,' I said snappily, 'Late, I expect I'll be working all bloody night,' I growled.

Josue looked sad, 'You see, it's my mother's birthday party and I would really like to lock up on time, just tonight that is. I usually sit in the caretaker's office and wait for the last person to leave, sometimes I don't even make it home as there's no point. But tonight is special.'

Josue looked so desperate I suggested that he gave me the keys and I would lock up and Josue had reluctantly handed them over and I had reassuringly nodded and implied I would be very responsible and lock everything up correctly.

'Shit, did I forget to lock up? Have all the homeless people in London now made the Wonder Fashion school their home? I started hyperventilating but then managed to pull it back and re-spool, no I clearly remembered locking each door as I went out. So, what happened after Josue left? I opened the first box. It was filled to the brim with old fashion magazines, newspaper clippings, sample swatches and other various accoutrements that I guess clothing empires collect on their journey through the fabric of life. I had picked up a copy of the 1950s' inspirational magazine for women "Wife". It featured a somewhat frothy article on underwear with advice on the correct kitchen, bedroom and dining under garment attire and on the opposite page a model was advertising the Wonder girdle.

The Wonder girdle was Bill Wonder's magnum opus and had launched Bill's thousand-million-pound empire. I nodded appreciatively at the clever spring tension design. What was the catchphrase? 'We can make the world a better place, one butt at a time.'

As I read the article, it occurred to me that I had never actually seen a Wonder Girdle in the flesh. This was odd especially considering I had come across hundreds of anthropometric Berlei Gay slants, Sasha's and Sarongsters whilst studying my degree in Fashion history and had also religiously rummaged through the VA clothing collection hundreds of times but had never come across a Wonder.

I studied the girdle illustrations and marvelled at its silhouette engineering with its 100% guarantee that once you were zipped in, your flesh wasn't going anywhere. To allow for some movement demonstrated by several diagrams of the girdle in action, woman with vacuum, woman hanging out washing, woman bending over, it was made out of nine overlapping panels which worked on a spring release movement. This also had the advantage of forcing the wearer to have a perky spring in her step every time movement was attempted. Thereby, according to the blurb, adding psychological and physiological benefits without the aid of medication.

'Maybe I should buy one,' I had muttered and then the heating vent made a sound a bit like,

'Maybe you should.'

I unfolded an old film poster of the famous blithesome, beautiful and spirited starlet Dora Duffy sitting on a bar stool, lips clenched presumably whistling her classic number, 'I feel so hot when you're around me.' Dora had managed to resolve the age-old female contradiction of Madonna or whore by wearing clothes that were tight enough to show she was a woman but loose enough to show she was a lady. I remembered watching the film in my fashion and film module at college, not only was it a box office hit but it served to highlight the moral as well as functional role of the correct undergarments. Angel, a cabaret singer, is sexually assaulted after the show in Hay's code montage of close ups of her mouth as she shouts 'no' at a shadowy outline in a trilby hat. Angel's husband Harry, a fine muscular hero type is so incensed he finds her assailant and bludgeons him to death with a gold statue of a falcon. He is arrested and the lawyer explains to Angel that if her husband stands any chance of an acquittal, she must wear the Wonder girdle at all times. Angel does as instructed and appears in court in a navy twin set with a white Bettina blouse and string bow tie. Given her heavily structured bullet bosom, tiny waist and limited stride, she is all importantly packed inside her Wonder girdle. Her staunchly controlled and bang on trend figure is all the jury needs and her husband is acquitted. After that the Wonder girdle sold like it was going out of style. I always particularly liked the little Abrahamic up yours in the last scene just before the credits when a box is delivered to the lawyer's office and when he opens it, he finds a Wonder girdle.

As my tube train screeched into Finsbury Park, I briefly wondered if my exposure to 1950s' product placement could have led to my suspension. No, I didn't think that was it, Bill was very keen on exposing his staff to all sorts of advertising. I tried to piece together what had happened after I opened the second box. The second box had several layers of tape wrapped around and after I cut through, I found it contained more personal stuff, an old leathery baseball glove, a faded sepia photograph circa 1910 of a young couple on their wedding day. He looked nervous in a charcoal top hat in hand and a flower in his buttonhole. His new wife wore a full-length wedding dress with a high collar and was holding a squat wedding bouquet of chrysanthemums.

Could this be Bill's mum and dad?

Next there was a photograph of a flighty, capricious woman standing in front of the New York Guggenheim dressed in a honeycomb swing coat with large white chocolate buttons and wide allsorts sleeves. She cast an ephemeral halo, possibly the result of intense colour saturation or maybe suggestive of some sort of phantasmagoria. Could this be Bill's first wife Hettie who had left him for a Cuban double bass player? I pondered the "great beauty" label fashion folklore had bestowed upon her. To my way of thinking she was too highly interbred, too high maintenance, emancipated and arched rather like the final consanguinity of a pairing between Marlene Dietrich and Vivien Leigh to claim such a title. But she certainly had a certain *technicolour je ne sais quoi* about her.

I put the Hettie photograph on top of the wedding photograph on my desk and rummaged around some more. A leather photograph album caught my eye and I was just about to open it when the lights in the office went out. This wasn't unusual as the lights worked on a movement sensor and if there weren't enough enthusiastic young people nervously running around, they would go out. What was rather odd was an accompanying popping noise like the sound of a Manalo high heel shoe snapping, followed by what sounded like, 'don't do it.'

As I was getting a bit freaked out and it was nearly 9 pm, I decided to pack up and work on the wall displays at home so I hastily swept all my marking into my new Chinese workers haute tote and diligently locked up. As my brain chittered in time with the tube's rolling stock, I had a worrying premonition and I walked back to my flat with a heavy doomed feeling which added a new layer of unease to my general workplace anxiety. I opened the door and slowly picked up my new Chinese workers' haute tote and emptied out the contents. The last three of the student's trend analysis assignments fell out first then the 1950s aspirational magazine "Wife" flopped out neatly folded on the Wonder girdle article. Lastly the heavy photograph album crashed to the floor in an insouciant there's-no-escaping-your-destiny kind of way.

I sat on the floor and eyed the photograph album suspiciously; was it the reason why I had been suspended? What secrets could it contain, could it shed light on Bill's rather sketchy past? Could it contain fashion cycle predictions, making money algorithms, secret codes on how to become a fashion billionaire?

Could it be Bill's Rosebud?

I was going to open it and take a peek but then decided to do the right thing and instead I rang HR in an attempt to clear the matter up before it went too far. It went straight into the answer phone. I was going to leave a message along the lines of, 'Sorry I didn't realise that I had taken the album and it really was an accident. I will bring it straight back,' but then I had a better idea. Well actually in hindsight it was a really crap idea, but it seemed like a good idea at the time. My simple and supposedly fool proof plan was to take the album back tomorrow morning and find Gita, apologise and convince her I hadn't looked inside. Then I had an even better idea, I could simply shove the album back in the box and say, 'Hey it was here all along, hurray, drama over. It's okay, it was just a mistake and I'm not an old family photo album thief. And I can't have looked in it either.'

The landline rang again; could it be Gita calling me back?

'Sadie, is that you?'

It was my grandmother, or Bubbe.

When I had last visited my Bubbe at her exorbitantly expensive nursing home, (I mean they just sit in chairs all day) she had warned me not to get involved with Bill Wonder. Bubbe was 94 and labelled doolally and almost all the chutzpah had been knocked out of her. 'Sadie,' she had cried when she noticed me, 'you're overdressed.'

This was a fair comment; to try and fit in at the school, I had been buying a lot of fake designer clothes in an attempt to disguise my social imposter anxiety.

'Bubbe,' I cried gratefully and in a rather surprised way as I didn't think she was up to phone calls any more.

'What's wrong Moon?' she replied using her pet name for me.

'Nothing,' I tried to sound breezy.

'Moon, what's that schnorrer done now?'

'Who?' I replied trying to play innocent but knowing full well that my grandmother was not a woman to hide things from.

'Bill Wonder.'

'Well, I guess I have been suspended.'

'What!,' she spat in disbelief, 'it was bad enough that my flesh and blood is working for that nogoodnik, gonef fat thief. But now he has suspended you, why? Did you kick him in the tuckus?'

'I'm not entirely sure Bubbe. I think it's because I accidentally took a photograph album,'

'Really,' said Bubbe sounding a little too excited, 'You finally have the book. You clever girl, Sadie, what did you do to get it? He wouldn't just give it to you, particularly you.'

'Well, I accidentally took it home.'

'Oy vey, really is that your story, yes keep to it, it was all one big accident.'

'But it's the truth,' I started to remonstrate.

'There's work to be done now you've got the book, but are you sure the time is right. Have the general public finally woken up, but yes you're young, I guess you know.' Bubbe stopped suddenly and I could hear her rasping to draw breath, in an 'I might have a stroke' kind of way.

I tried to calm Bubbe down and thinking she had misunderstood me said, 'Bubbe, I think it's an old photograph album, probably of Bill's family but I haven't looked in it yet. I was going to take it back.'

Bubbe bellowed, 'What, take it back, take it back she says, now now I'm 94, you say take it back, what you think, I'm going to live another ten years.'

'But I think it's why I've been suspended,' I reasoned.

'You think, you think, Sadie do you think I don't know exactly who the fat shapeless ferreter is? I'm not like your generation, having to look at phones to remember. No, I have memories and I know who Wonder is. I used to dress him.'

17

Bubbe stopped suddenly and wheezed dramatically and I decided to change the subject quickly.

'Bubbe, how was your lunch?' I replied hastily.

This evidently did not work as Bubbe replied, 'Sadie, do you remember the shop in Plymouth with all those fat shlumpers? Oh Vey, it was a challenge trying to dress them, not like my corset franchise at Dapplewhites, not at all.'

'Yes, of course, I remember Bubbe,' I replied in a soothing tone.

'Do you remember when you spent the summers with me and you helped out in the shop?'

'Yes, Bubbe, I loved it,' I replied.

'And then we would go home and make coconut macaroons and almond balls. And I told you stories about my lingerie workshop in the East End.'

'Yes, I remember, Bubbe,' I answered, aware that I have not successfully diverted the topic.

'My Silver workshop made the best slimming and flattering undergarments in the whole of London. Mr Dapplewhite, the owner of Dapplewhites department store told me that, do you remember Sadie?'

'Sort of.'

'Then we had to move,' she shouted down the telephone angrily. 'Then I was so embarrassed and we had to rrrrun. Get out of London quick before we were labelled. We had to move to Devon because of that shapeless slippery gonef. Is he dead yet? I can't hold out much longer but I'll see him out if it's the last thing I do.'

'Okay Bubbe, but it doesn't matter now,' I placated.

'Doesn't it, Sadie, doesn't it matter anymore? Have you finally got the schnorrer then?' she asked naively.

'Maybe,' I soothed.

'I remember dancing at the Astoria off Oxford Street, that's where I met your pops. We must go dancing there one day Sadie. Shall I knock you up a Schiaparelli?'

'Yes please, Bubbe. Make it the lobster dress and I might catch myself a king,' I replied, relieved I had calmed her down.

'Sadie, you are the wrong sex for that king. Now be a good girl and run along. I must be off to the shop now. Those shop girls can't do anything without me,' she added sleepily.

'Okay Bubbe, I will see you soon,' I said, blowing her a kiss down the phone.

'Sadie remember, petty thieves are hung, big ones are pardoned,' she added and the phone went dead.

Chapter 2
Overedge Stitch

Early the next morning, I dressed in one of my grandmother's Chanel Comeback collection 1953 tweed suits, which I had to say went brilliantly with my new look and put the 'Wife' magazine and the photograph album in my bag. As I walked out the door, I had a transient nagging doubt about ignoring my grandmother's advice but after a final glance in the hall mirror, which confirmed that I really was rocking my new retro look, I decided to keep to my do the right thing plan.

'What I really need is a matching bag and shoes,' I sighed. 'Oh well, fashion fades, style remains,' I added more positively.

I got out at Warren Street and nodded at the sushi shop manager, who was shouting at a man holding a large piece of raw fish, and then snuck around the back of the fashion school and inconspicuously let myself in the backdoor. The school was eerily empty and as I walked up the stairs to the eighth-floor office, there was a very strong smell of paper glue and wee.

When I got to my desk, the boxes had gone. Whilst I stood indecisively pondering my next move, I glanced out of the window and spotted Bill on the balcony. He had his back to me and appeared to be talking to someone but I couldn't see who. He also, very oddly for him, had a very downcast slant to his shoulders. Usually he strode around his kingdom, well fashion school, as if he was king of the world, which to be fair he kind of was but today he seemed to have lost his cocksure arrogant veneer. Also oddly, given his ennui, he looked taller and slimmer than usual, not really broad and tubby at all.

My first instinct was to hide, maybe squat down behind my desk before he had noticed me. But then I stopped, dare I tell him I was bringing the photograph album back and I haven't looked inside. No probably not. We underling workers implicitly understood that we must not engage in conversation with Bill unless he elicited it first. Then Bill unexpectedly turned in my direction and I wasn't quick enough to assume my usual deferential head down position and instead I stood petrified to the spot, too scared to even blink. Bill looked at me and I looked at him. I wasn't sure if my innate terror came across as defiance but instead of being chastised, something near miraculous happened. Bill didn't look angry or annoyed. He didn't mouth through the window, 'I'll have your head for this.' He looked terrified, truly and utterly petrified. As if he had finally met his nemesis.

This range of emotions completely confused me and I was a little offended, as I didn't think my new look was that bad but I was rather enjoying my totally unexplained, elevated position in this power play. I bravely gave him a stern look as I slowly backed away. I had to stop retreating when I banged into the door of the plant room storage area but I think I still managed to pull off dignified insolence as I coolly unlocked it with Josue's keys and closed it tightly behind me before daring to take a breath out. As I stood behind the door feeling completely flummoxed, I heard Jonathan from visual design approaching the staffroom chirpily singing, 'Fashion, I love fashion.'

I briefly remembered that Jonathan said he always got to work early, something about his childhood. Then the building shook violently and I lost my footing and fell hard against the doorframe. As I rebalanced, I felt a bit chintzy. Bill's odd stricken face, the preceding events, and Jonathan's unself conscious singing had completely unhinged me. Was I now to be labelled a thief and a billionaire scarer? Was the building's subsidence problem my fault as well?

Then I heard a series of pitchy screams. I tentatively opened the door and saw Jonathan standing by the balcony door. He was wearing his 'I'm beyond shocked' look. A look usually reserved for camel toe, orange skin, and tweed slacks. The rest of the staff was now tottering into the office in a clutter of high heel shoes, designer jeans, and glittery tops.

'Good grief, what is it man?' blustered Mags Twill from Buying heaving herself over to the balcony.

'Not a pretty woman,' I sighed. 'How she ended up in fashion is one of life's great mysteries.'

Alice, the personal shopping teacher, was now also looking down, 'It looks like a bundle of discarded men's suits, most likely off the peg but it's hard to tell when you're looking down from above.'

'Yes it's an off the peg grey suit alright,' replied Maggie Cotton, the pattern cutting and design teacher 'and it's contorted around something very flat and under stretchered.'

'Could it be one of Jonathan's shop mannequins?' Mags Twill said hesitantly.

'No, my mannequins are all thin and lithe with perfect symmetrical features; this mannequin looks short and rather tubby.' Jonathan replied in an affronted manner.

Then Maggie Cotton rasped in her old punk accent, 'It's Bill… it must be Bill, I recognise the phone.'

Maggie Cotton's eye for detail is second to none; she can recognise a stitch in time. The phone – retro, vintage, can one still say old, was Bill's trademark and if the phone was next to the compressed mannequin, she could be right.

Alice squealed, 'Mags C is right, Bill Wonder is lying on the forecourt below. His body is rather asymmetrical though, like, like, like a diagrammatic Haring T-shirt.'

'I would like to know how he got there,' huffed Mags Twill.

'I guess he could have been the victim of a hit and run whilst walking the two yards from his limousine to the school doors,' replied Alice helpfully.

'Or he could have been attacked by a vendetta charged businessman?' replied Alistair.

'An insulted student?' interjected Maggie Cotton.

'A bulimic ex-fashion model?' Jonathan added.

'A cheated-out-of-their-pension aggrieved employee?' Mags Twill added knowingly.

They all nodded.

Jonathan looked down and then at the balcony and added thoughtfully, 'Do you think Bill fell from the balcony?'

'Pushed, more like,' added Mags Twill ominously.

'Is he dead?' whispered Alice nervously winding her golden curls around her finger.

'How the hell should I know,' Mags Twill snapped.

Alice let out a sob and her armadillos sagged.

'There's a group of students down there. I wonder if they saw what happened,' suggested Jonathan helpfully. 'They must have screamed but what are they doing now?'

'Umm, I think some are checking their hairdos are still intact, and some are filming Bill's body on their phones,' answered Maggie Cotton who was now leaning perilously over the balcony.

'In a few minutes, the whole incident will saturate social media and Bill's crushed body will be trending worldwide,' Alice said whimsically.

'Perhaps famous people need to think about this. If you're famous and happen to die in a public place, the whole world can see your dead body within minutes,' Mags Twill said pondering this like a maths calculation. 'I actually don't think Bill would be that bothered, he was clearly never a vain man, but what about all those female celebrities? Celebrities whose careers have been made or lost based on a strand of hair. How would blood splattered and broken on a grey paving stone play out?'

'We, the general public, would take one look and say, she really wasn't that pretty after all. I really never liked her and look at her hair, it's just a little too dishevelled and her mascara seems to have run. Obviously, a has-been. Over. Who's next?' agreed Maggie Cotton.

Mags Twill suddenly shouted, 'Wait has anyone called an ambulance?'

It really didn't seem likely.

Mags Twill called the emergency services. 'Everyone, follow me now,' she commanded.

Everyone clattered after her. Mags Twill, leading her patrol, a group of lecturers in fashion design, fashion buyers, merchandising and styling. Yes, they certainly were the "go to" people in an emergency. To give Jonathan some credit, if he had been first at the scene, he could have used his visual display flair to arrange Bill in a more aesthetically pleasing way.

Tanya stilettoed out of her office. 'Where are you going?' she asked, surprised.

'I think Bill's dead,' sniped Mags Twill.

Tanya let out a high staccato laugh, a laugh that said 'could my dreams have finally come true?' She then looked at the staff; presumably someone managed to pull off concern. I was wondering why she was wearing a tight scaly blue sheath that made her look like a Minke whale. When she realised that this wasn't some flippant fashion comment about our dictatorial megalomaniac boss, but possibly something that was actually true, she joined the patrol and they bunkered on, handbags drawn.

As the staffroom emptied, I felt a huge sense of relief and instinctively stretched out my tightly wound arms. My momentarily lack of cognisance had disastrous consequences as I knocked over a mannequin wearing a green velvet 'Gone with the Wind' ball gown with a bang on trend ripped bodice. As I watched her slow-mo to the floor, I wondered whether I was to be undone by a shoddily made 2018 simulacrum copy of a 1940s' simulacrum copy of a circa 1862 American Civil War curtain statement dress. No, I decided I will not be beaten by a meaningless postmodern slip and I ran towards the plant room fire exit and gave the door a hard shove. Something on the other side was blocking it and it won't budge.

'Oh shit,' I wailed, as I bounced off the door.

I wondered whether I could just hide out in the plant room forever but I did rather suspect that a dead billionaire would lead to some sort of search of the building. Then I noticed something grey and shiny at the far end of the plant room.

'It must be the tradesmen lift,' I said gawking in wonder.

I had heard about the tradesmen lift. Jonathan had spoken about it. But I had never seen it. Bill used it of course, used it to move stealthily between floors. Used it to appear as if by magic and shout at you when you least expected it. But I had never been able to trace its origin. Now it made sense. It must start here in the plant room, then pass through the large store cupboard at the back of the sewing room, through the back of Jonathon's visual design studio and then down past Bill's newly refurbished office before finishing on the ground floor near the caretaker's office at the back of the building.

I blindly raced across the spongy grey carpet only to bash into a hat stand covered in a powdery white substance. The hat stand wobbled precariously and several Lily Dache flower petal hats fluttered down on me followed by a swarm of black clothes hangers which dived angrily at my face. I took refuge behind a stack of packing boxes and waited for the swarm to pass. I had a few painful scratches and blood was dripping from my forehead.

I took a deep breath, 'Nearly there now,' I muttered resolutely and then the packing boxes collapsed under my weight and a pool of pale-green polystyrene foam packing beads cascaded over me. The polystyrene beads quickly covered me in a soupy overcoat and I felt very tempted to just throw in the towel and await my fate in this not uncomfortable cool plastic flotation tank but I began to sense I wasn't alone. Something with more backbone was slithering through the polystyrene and it felt spookily like a large snake and whilst drowning in a spongy polymerisation packing case mire held a certain Pre-Raphaelite appeal, doing so with a slimy feather Boa crushing me to death did not. I slowly wrenched myself out and made a grab for a clothes rail full of dusty black and white twin sets which slid to the floor. As the twinsets landed roughly, they bravely seem to sing out Chanel's glib unattainable philosophy,

'Just be yourself.'

The accompanying soundtrack of my journey across the plant room must have reverberated around the whole building and I was very aware that I needed to escape and quickly. I dragged myself a few more steps to the lift shaking off beads and feathers and blood and broken bits of clothes hangers and pressed the down button.

Nothing happened.

'Now what?' I whimpered lamely and then I remembered what Jonathan had said, 'You need a key to operate the tradesmen lift.'

I hastily looked through the bunch of keys Josue had given me, none fitted. I tried irrationally pleading with the lift; please, please, just open, please, please.' This didn't work on my cold-hearted steed. Then I noticed a pair of Chanel two tone black and beige slingbacks on the shelf next to the lift. They were just what I needed to finish my outfit. As I reached greedily for the shoes, a key box hidden behind them opened automatically and a shiny silver key with the words OTIS and the serial number 001958 fell out.

'A woman with good shoes is never ugly,' I said whilst chirpily putting the shoes on and slotting the key into the lift door. As I triumphantly re-slung my ironic, "I'm not a shopping bag" bag, I felt the weight of the photograph album digging into my ribs. Fate or timing had stopped us from parting company so far but I still hadn't actually opened it. If I did, I was unsure what requisite duties would follow, but I was pretty certain things would get worse before they got better... if they got better.

I looked at the album and pensively hopped from foot to foot. 'Should I or shouldn't I, should I or shouldn't I,' I chanted hesitantly.

'No, don't do it,' the heating pipes groaned.

Chapter 3
Obsolescence

The square was packed when I tentatively opened the back door. The unfolding scene was reminiscent of a Hieronymus Bosch Middle Ages doom painting, with some added extra-pigmented pastel-coloured sumptuary apparel. Central to the composition was Bill, now rather artfully draped and framed in several pink Wonder Empire sweatshirts. Bill's short, fat, pink outline had a quasi-religious quality – the clothing messiah brought low, surrounded by an army of fashionistas, paramedics, policemen, B list celebrities, tourists, the homeless and even a few shadowy skeletons.

Skeletons! I was mystified, could the gates of hell have opened whilst I was stuck in the plant room? Had Armageddon befallen the western world? If it had, I have to say the souls from the other side were really rather polite and clearly believed in queuing.

'Have they been sent to collect Bill?' I gasped. 'Of course, a pact with the devil or supernatural dealing would explain it all.'

One of the dead (or were they undead), bumped into me and as I quickly put my head down to avoid detection, I noticed she had a price tag pinned to her shoulder. She also looked familiar; in fact, she looked very much like Becca, a student from visual design.

'It's really flattering isn't it,' she said to another skeleton, 'Luckily I found the last size four in the van,' she said whilst pointing to a Wonder Empire delivery van, its back doors jacked wide open.

'Yes, it is, they must have A/W dress,' replied the skeleton who I think was in merchandising, 'they may be poorly made copies of an Elsa Schiaparelli skeleton dress, but the factory got the boning right.'

'I know,' replied Becca. 'The van driver was trying to deliver them to Wonder's flagship shop Best Girl on Oxford Street before you lot stopped it.'

'We decided to stage a mini fashion revolution now that the king is dead,' laughed the other skeleton. 'So we put down our means of production, well, stopped writing assignments and broke ranks and raided the vault, well, van.'

'Viva the revolution,' Becca replied. 'Do you want some of this *Day of the Dead* makeup. It's meant for shop mannequins but it gives human skin a really cool ghostly, supernatural glow.'

'No, I'm okay, thanks,' said the skeleton jauntily, throwing the matt white pan in the air as she and Becca walked away.

As I hid behind the industrial bins, I looked for a possible escape route. I spotted Tanya contorting with indecisiveness. Her eyes jersey-stitching uncontrollably as she muttered to herself, 'What should I do, what should I do? Surely Bill's head office has a protocol for this, surely he would have insisted we knew it.'

Finally, she went from panic to decisiveness. 'We must call the emergency services,' she cried.

Mags Twill who was always quick off the mark to prove she was the most capable person in the room, fired back, 'It's already been done, I rang about 10 minutes ago and I can hear them now.'

Tanya deflated, her lack of what to do-ness palpable as she looked around helplessly. Fortunately, the French rose to her aid. Geneviève aged 36 and the new head of finance, assumed responsibility. Geneviève was stylish in that French way, slim, unruffled and able to pull off stripes and patterns. She spoke up, her silken voice cutting through the Essex twang, 'Please, if you may, can employees please move away from the body, I mean the … him … er … Mr Wonder.'

The fashion students looked up from their orderly queues, but didn't move. A thought must have threaded in Genevieve's head, could Bill still be alive? No one had actually checked.

'Does anyone know about first aid?' Genevieve asked tentatively.

No one came forward. Then one of the students piped up that she was an A&E nurse before she developed a passion for fashion. She checked his pulse and made a slight nod of her head. At that moment the paramedics pushed their way through the crowd but stopped when they came to Bill's body and shook their heads knowingly. There was a pregnant pause, as it slowly washed over the staff, the students, the gathering homeless and several tourists that Bill Wonder was definitely dead and there was to be no sudden heart stopping suspense, followed by a miraculous Bill resurrection. No Kiss of Life to the tune of Nellie the Elephant or Staying Alive; no adrenaline injections in the heart, not even a ballpoint pen in his neck.

This great anticlimactic act resulted in lack of interest, even boredom on the spectators' behalf. As the students went back to their phones, I tentatively stepped out but any thought of escape was thwarted by hundreds of police cars speeding into Alfred Square. As I stood pin-cushioned to the spot, I could see a police car heading straight for the glass windows at the front of the fashion school where several students had huddled on the pavement smoking fags. If the police car continued on its trajectory, it would crush them against their castle of fashion dreams. Was I about to witness the second tragedy of the day? I could cry out and warn them but I was conflicted. If I did, I might be recognised and it would be game over for me.

My callous thought process shocked me. Had I become a psychopath, so focused on the end game that I was prepared to lose a few young fashionistas, like pawns in a game of chess? Fortunately, I didn't have to test my lack of empathy further as the police car stopped just shy of the students. I stepped further back and hunched down. As the new world order of uniforms started to populate in the fashion square, the gender divide was obvious, fashionistas were girls or gay boys who were now furiously spraying perfume, applying lip gloss and practising sexy nonchalant poses. Emergency services were boys who clearly liked fast modes of transport, uniforms and holding long hard phallic shaped weapons.

As old-fashioned style masculinity spooled out from the emergency services. I noticed Tanya breathe a sigh of relief and mutter, 'Sod fluidity of gender identity. I need a big posturing man to take control of this huge tangled mess.'

She put on her disarming smile and made a bee line over to a strapping young policeman. She tapped him on the shoulder and thrust her right hand out in preparation for a firm handshake.

'I'm Tanya Robinson, principal of the fashion ....'

Tanya stopped; the policeman was ignoring her and doing something with red and white tape. He looked up nervously and said, 'Please move away from the crime scene, ma'am.'

Tanya stepped back. She wasn't used to being ignored. She was Bill's right hand woman and was known for her ball-breaking persona. She could make a whole department cry in under five minutes and had allegedly made three work experience students wet themselves with fear on the same day. The young policeman seemed immune to her charm and I could tell she was perplexed. She tried pouting which may have worked when she was younger but now made her appear high on opioids. The young policeman was still entirely indifferent. Tanya reached over and tapped him on the shoulder again. As he straightened up, he flicked his hair and did a Pacino "are you looking at me" stare and I heard several skeletal fashionistas go 'mmmm.'

The female gaze was abruptly broken by the arrival of the Buying students. Everyone at the fashion school knows not to mess with the Buyers. Trained by Mags Twill and overseen by Bill they were an unstoppable, merciless force. Armed with their homogenous attractive uniform of blond hair extensions, fake tan and Samsonite suitcases, they had been taught to think nothing of flying to India and badgering a factory owner into a price reduction, knowing that the repercussions of this would result in a village starving to death. Profit was all they had been trained to care about. A 400% mark-up was their mantra. Never mind the quality, feel the width was their religion.

They were, in short, the life blood of the Wonder Empire and as long as they made money, were untouchable. But one too many fake rips on a skinny, camouflage green when emerald was in, a batch of onesies with orangutan hair that didn't sell and they were out. Bill Wonder hated to lose money; an unaccounted-for fiver could send him into a rage for a week. An unsold range of clothes would usually mean that the unfortunate buyer who had signed off on it would never work in fashion again.

Harvey Dickens, Mags Twill's most aspiring protégé, a tall, lean, white, hussar like creature, clearly destined for a great trend related exploitive career, had lined up his troop of Home Countries trending (currently Indian stripper or sexy cowgirl) junior Buyers behind him as he spoke to Tanya.

'Well he could have fallen, but he was short and fat. He really would have had to stand on the first rail, maybe he was looking over, maybe Kate or Cara walked past, and maybe he was waving. OMG – maybe they were dissing him and he was like angry, waving and shouting. Do you think they have refused to be in his next advert; if they're not in it, what will happen, who will buy the clothes?'

As the fledgling Buyers patiently waited for their leader, they made Midwich Cuckoo brooding eyes at the young policeman and then started to slowly move in on him. The policeman looked up startled. He was just about to put a torn piece of heavy black material into an "I love shopping" bag which a kindly fashionista had handed him. As the policeman backed away from the Buyers, he bumped into Harvey and a few of Harvey's disciples giggled.

Harvey wasn't a young man that liked to be laughed at and he gave his followers a look, a look that would ordinarily have your opponent doubting whether they had put deodorant on or worse, had something trapped in their teeth. But the young Buyers didn't look worried. They looked defiant. Did they know that Harvey's reign was about to end? Harvey looked flouncy and was no doubt about to say something cutting when the policeman abruptly moved Harvey to the side. The coltish Buyers giggled again. Harvey looked incensed but the PC pointed to the ground. Harvey was standing very near to Bill's body and by the look on his face, he had just realised that the creamy white lump at his foot was Bill's brain matter. The up and coming Buyers giggled again and Harvey looked desperate and dangerous.

The Square was now overrun with emergency services, students, tourists and the homeless and I started to feel very uneasy. As I tried to slink further back, I stumbled over a rather large Timmy Toe stiletto shoe which was lying pairless on the pavement. I instinctively put it in my tote.

The police were taking down names of witnesses. They looked confused as if they didn't really believe young people have names like Rolex, Chanel, Diamante and Twinkle. A police photographer appeared.

'Look at the size of his camera,' laughed one of the Buyers.

The photographer was trying his best to take photos of the crime scene but young fashionistas kept popping into shot pulling Facebook faces. Girls; toss of the mane, chin down eyes up. Boys; facing camera, direct stare into lens, wry smile.

The pathologist arrived and unveiled Bill's body. Most people had forgotten Bill was still there; a short round bundle of pink billionaire. The photographer was instructed what to photograph and then the pathologists placed plastic bags over Bill's head, feet and hands. The Buyers recoiled and I heard Harvey's ex best friend Twinkle say, 'Like how does that work as a look? I even feel a bit sorry for him. Make sure they never put a plastic bag over my head if I'm dead.'

A 4-door saloon arrived and as other lesser steeds cleared space for it, I guessed this must be the detective. I sneaked a surreptitious glance at the man in charge. He wasn't the "vast colossus of a man"; he "who doth bestride the narrow world" sort of guy. He was rather slight, old and quite frankly, rather knackered looking. It was a bit like when you meet a film star in real life and discover they are 5 ft 4 inches. He was clearly one of those men who'd renounced looking pretty, born at a time when fashion belonged to women not men. He was a man who had worn a grey suit (probably the same style of grey suit) throughout his whole career. This lack of engagement with fashion made me wonder if he might not understand how things work at the Wonder Fashion School. The school was the very beating heart of the fashion retail bonanza, the "built-in my image" shrine to Bill Wonder's capitalist empire. This detective might misread the subtleties of fashion capitalism, not notice its pattern and layout. He could entirely underestimate the power of the fashion industry and its ability to maintain the hegemonic status quo.

This I found very reassuring, very reassuring indeed.

The paramedics put Bill's body into the ambulance and drove away. Bill had finally left the building, the street, the empire.

No one cried or even cared.

I realised that although it would have been easy to sneak away from self-obsessed fashionistas, it might not be as easy with the whole of the London Met watching and I started to panic. Any one of a hundred people could say, 'What are you doing here?' and I would be exposed as an imposter and potential murderer.

My grandmothers' warning kept darting through my head, 'No good will come of working with that gonef, Wonder.'

I was breathing shallow, panic-attack breaths, which was making me feel dizzy and light headed and I was well aware I could be uncovered at any moment unless I found a better hiding place. I saw a tatty rolled-up sleeping bag poking out between the bins, so I reached out, pulled it straight and crawled in. As I lay under the musty sleeping bag trying to think of a way of escaping, I noticed a bundle of raggedy clothes wedged at the bottom. I surreptitiously rummaged through my hands shaking and pulled out a bowler hat, a walking stick and some incredibly long fake eyelashes, which

I was fairly certain had been used for the Clockwork Orange, anti-knife crime window display in May. I had happened upon a double layer of disguise and I felt weak with relief.

Much to my surprise, I discovered a giant fat tear on my check as I added the eyelashes. Could this be because I'm exiled, friendless and trying to avoid getting arrested for the murder of a billionaire by hiding in a sleeping bag behind an industrial bin, wearing a wilfully retro 1950s Chanel comeback suit, which debatably could be sartorially interpreted as empowering but now that I've accessorised it with a bowler hat, walking stick and fake eyelashes, has lost all reference points? No, I was way beyond caring.

Could it be for Bill? Maybe, his death today added a whole new layer of complications and indeed implications that I really hadn't bargained for when I left home this morning.

Could it be for the as yet unclarified knights' errand I was about to embark on?

Yes, certainly, but it didn't completely address my melancholy. I think what finally tipped the balance was the tapestry unfolding in front of me; the predestined undoing of the bovver booted crusade that my Sisyphus feminist sisters-in-law had worked so hard to achieve. What a waste of punk women, I sniffed self-pityingly.

I peeked out from my feathery camouflage, the Princess Lisa pub was just to the right of my current destination. And then remembered, if you walked past the lavatories to the end of the narrow corridor with its colourful, tiled panels and mosaic floor, there was a back door which leads onto Grape Street and then back onto Oxford Street.

Could I escape through it and get the tube home and lie in bed and pretend I knew nothing when the police called. I decided to make a dash for it and was going to scurry over as inconspicuously as I could when I remembered the Coco Chanel quote, 'Keep your heels, head and standards high,' and instead strolled over to the pub in a queen-of-the-world way. My escape plan was undone as soon as I opened the door.

Despite the pub being mostly empty, it was only just after 9 am after all. The only table that was occupied was the long oblong table that ran along the mirrored back wall next to the back corridor. It was occupied by the staff huddled in a contemporary night watch, bathed in a jaundiced light cast by the sun shining onto the mustard tiles. The only way I could execute my escape plan was by following the path of black and white floor tiles around the marble effect island bar, with its mirrored Corinthian capitals. If any of the staff somehow managed to miss my actual body, they could catch glimpses of me from every conceivable mirrored angle as I tiptoed past. *Damn the gin palace style,* I thought despondently.

The barman was looking worried by my arrival and you could tell he was thinking, *If I let one of them in, one of the mad, bad or dispossessed, more are bound to follow.* Left with a Hobson's choice of malediction outside the pub or condemnation with the potential of a pint of Guinness inside, I chose to stay. I sat behind an etched-glass-panelled snob screen and did my best to earwig the staff gossip. I assumed the identity of a very important person who just happened to be passing before my next performance, possibly in a modern interpretation of a Shakespearean play. My lost thespian approach worked well as the barman came over with a freshly poured pint, and said whilst coughing in a hacking way, 'Have this on me love, you look like you need it – but don't tell your friends, unless they're celebrities.'

I gave him a queen-like wave and gratefully supped my hoboed ale. 'What's happening over there,' he asked, 'Is Bill Wonder dead?'

'Yes, think so,' I replied in a muffled way as I didn't want any of my colleagues hearing me.

'Did one of his enemies finally get him?'

'I've no idea,' I replied.

'Do you work there; you look sort of familiar?'

'Maybe,' I clipped.

'I'm not sure if I should say anything, but there was a group of Japanese, I'm not sure what, Ninjas I think – in here a few days ago,' he whispered confidentially, 'they sort of stood out. Not the usual crowd, although my clientele is rather varied.'

'Ninjas,' I said incredulously and a bit too loudly.

'Well, they weren't dressed like ninjas, dressed in rather beautiful charcoal suits made of some expensive material but they moved very quietly and seemed to appear and reappear but maybe that's the mirror panelled trick of the light. They did spend a long time looking at the Wonder school and writing notes down as if they were working stuff out.'

I nodded out of politeness but was more interested in trying to overhear the staff.

The staff had lined up about four drinks each. The barman noticed me peering over at them, 'Yes, I would say they are in shock but really, they drink like that most days, guess it's an occupational habit.'

The staff were knocking them back and eyeing each other nervously, funny what a potential killer can do to group dynamics.

'So, who killed Bill then,' thundered Mags Twill.

'I can come up with a top twenty before I finish my pint,' said Jonathan.

'More like a top 200,' said Maggie Cotton dryly.

'It could be the ghost. The students and I often hear and sometimes see her,' said Alice whose eyes shone a little too much.

'Err in the real world,' interrupted Mags Twill, 'my money's on Tanya. Bill baited her every opportunity he got. She was like a wound-up broken orangutan after every meeting she had with him,' she chortled cruelly. 'I remember meetings, if you could call them that. Bill just shouted things like, "how much money have you lost now, you stupid woman." It really was nasty to watch. She started crying once and he said if I wanted a blubbering buffoon, I would have brought one.'

'She was wound so tight, it wouldn't have taken much to make her snap,' Maggie Cotton added, 'would have only taken one tiniest thing, an unwound bobbin thread to have her push her nightmares off the balcony.'

They all nodded for once in agreement.

Unusually Jonathan, the opinion leader, was quiet and looked guilty of something, probably not murder I speculated – but something.

'Has anyone seen Spooks today,' he nervously asked. Everyone signalled no.

'Who is Spooks, by the way?' asked Maggie Cotton.

'She's Jonathon's latest protégé,' jeered Mags Twill, 'she's that student, the sort of smelly hobo girl who clearly has problems. Oh Jonathon, you didn't let Spooks sleep in the mannequin cupboard, did you?'

Jonathan nodded.

'You mean your psychopath's dream cupboard. The one that's full of the arms, legs, trunks and heads of perfect dismembered plastic women – someone sleeps in there?' rasped Maggie Cotton.

'Yes,' replied Jonathan, 'she's homeless and I didn't want her to sleep on the streets. I am a bit worried about her mental state though. She loves sleeping in that cupboard and every morning as a thank you, she arranges the mannequin limbs into macabre body part installations for me.'

Mags Twill was shaking her head in an Olivier Hardy "that's another fine mess" way.

'I don't know where she is today,' continued Jonathon, 'but I noticed there was no body part installation.'

'Do you think Bill Wonder is today's body part installation?' said Alice with morbid excitement. 'Like has she moved on to actual bodies rather than mannequins? Bill was arranged in a rather diagrammatic Haring way. I've no idea what a person looks like when they hit the ground from eight floors up, but he was quite splayed out in a rather stylised arrangement and he was missing a shoe.'

'Don't be ridiculous,' snapped Mags Twill, 'she wouldn't have had time to arrange him. You'd better tell the police though.'

'I know,' Jonathan sighed. 'She seemed so promising when I interviewed her, she turned up in a heavily patterned polyester dress and smelt of wee. And she even told me to fuck off when I asked her the where do you see yourself in ten years' time question.'

'If she did kill him,' Alice added looking wild-eyed with cheap wine and fear, 'if she killed him and you let her in, are you like an accessory or something?'

'I don't know,' Jonathan said miserably.

'They will probably sack you at the very least,' gasped Alice.

'There, there, it will all be fine, you'll see,' Alistair, Jonathon's right-hand man soothed in a Renfield to Dracula way.

Jonathan gave him a look.

'Where's Sadie?' Mags Twill interrupted sensing it was time to change the subject before Jonathan did one of his angry verbal conflagrations.

'We can't mention Sadie's name or contact her, she's done something really bad. HR won't say what. But I suppose at least she can't be blamed for this,' answered Josue.

Josue from facilities was sitting very quietly, slightly away from the rest of the staff nervously rotating a set of keys through his hands like awkward rosary beads. 'She worked late,' he said, 'Tanya was making her do stuff and yesterday morning I heard Gita on the phone telling her she was suspended.'

'Why?' they asked in unison.

'I have no idea,' Josue replied, tightening his grip on one of the keys and forcing it into his knuckle.

'For that matter, where's Trixie?' asked Mags Twill suspiciously. 'Unlike her to have a day off. She's never off.'

'Maybe she did it,' said Jonathan nonchalantly. 'Have you noticed she's wearing even more terrible clothes recently? Why doesn't she get it, short, snub people can't wear feathers? She probably did it you know. If anyone was more stressed than Tanya, it was Trixie. Bill probably said something, like why are you dressed like a dodo and she went for him.'

Once again, the staff seemed to agree.

The detective entered the pub and I slunk lower on the barstool. He stopped and gasped. I had to admit the staff looked disturbing, like a collection of the worst horror film misfit extras ever. All smudged lipstick, pale yellowish faces, underground frizzy hair and crackly on edge conversation. Jonathan was holding a cigarette on a jaunty angle and slurring his words. He was pointing at Maggie Cotton and saying, 'Did I tell you the story of the UM bag.'

Mags Twill pulled an exasperated face, 'Yes, yes, yes, about a hundred times,' she snapped.

The detective approached. 'Please can you make your way back to the school.'

The staff ignored him. Mags Twill was now shouting and banging her fist in the slops, 'It's all balderdash, balderdash really, who killed Bill, who cares who killed him? We all hated him; we all could have killed him.'

The detective pushed forward and bellowed in a menacing game show voice, 'Ladies and gentlemen, make your way back to the office,' and then after breathing in, 'Nowwww.'

This got their attention and they got up and started to roll out of the pub.

Mags Twill hurried to the loo. She looked and moved like a shlumper. My grandmother had taught me about shlumpers when I was a child. Bubbe was always immaculately dressed usually in a Chanel twinset with pearls and matching accessories. Her hair tightly coiffured. Her face colour-keyed peaches and creams, and Hazel Bash kiss proof lips. Bubbe's brow would wrinkle when the poorly dressed, old-before-their-time farmers' wives entered her ladies Outfitters in Devon but she would assess each one thoroughly. She could always tell their exact measurements. Often just to prove she was right, she would send me to measure up. 'I made corsets for 30 years, Sadie,' she would say. 'There isn't a body shape in the world that I can't guess correctly.'

Most of Bubbe's new clients, unlike her London customer base, were too tired and worn-out by the daily grind to worry about their appearance and sought sensible, long-lasting, unprofitable clothes. Bubbe would look at me and say disparagingly, 'Look at all the shlumpers.' Sometimes Bubbe would see some potential in a shlumper and would take the farmer's wife and dress them like a Hollywood starlet. But most of the time she would shake her head and say, 'Sadie, there's no point. Don't waste your life beating on a wall, hoping to transform it into a door.'

I think Bubbe might have stepped forward to look at Mags Twill but then she would have had second thoughts and steered her towards the polyester florals. I guess Mags Twill didn't need Bubbe to tell her this; her disappointment was cross-stitched over her face. Her upper middle-class pedigree and red brick university should have led her straight up the corporate ladder but this had now snaked away and she now looked like she always felt one step away from where she should be. I heard her sigh as she prepared for the trek to the loo. I supped my beer and checked my bag, yes, the photo album was still firmly and incriminatingly weighing it down.

As the staff were now making their way back to the office, I could finally exit through the narrow corridor. I finished my pint and stood up, as I stepped over the black tiles the barman coughed, 'Love, the back door's locked. The police told me to lock it in case the murderer tries to escape through it.'

I had forgotten Mags Twill was still in the loo and as I turned, we almost collided. I did a sudden ducking down movement and my bowler hat slipped over my eyes and I gave Mags Twill an Alex from Clockwork Orange demonic look. She recoiled, startled and hurried out to find her tribe. The barman gave me an even more curious stare and I felt the only thing to do now was to follow Mags Twill out.

Chapter 4
Fashions, Not Fashion

The Square was even busier than before and I had to push my way through the urban Maslowian crowd. Tanya wrapped in a white faux fur polar bear coat which should have been glamorous, was standing on the steps of the school with a loud hailer.

'Will all students please go home, there is nothing to see. Please go home.'

I tried to head towards Gower Street but it soon became very apparent that all exits were blocked by officials taking down names and addresses. When it finally dawned on me that I was trapped, I stopped pushing and listened to snippets of conversations instead.

'I used to have a crush on Bill... well his money, because he was old and ugly.'

'Yeah the eight billion did make him very fanciable.' Her friend agreed.

'It's amazing that he did have so much money.'

'I guess, but when you think about it, a day doesn't pass without Bill's trends appearing somewhere in the media.'

'Arhh, the fashion cycle,' piped one of the homeless.

'Stylistic obsolescence,' shouted another.

'You what, mate,' hawked a journalist.

'It means throwing clothes away before you need to because they just don't look right anymore. Soon we will wear something once, and then throw it away,' replied his mate.

As I listened, I appreciated how Bill had created the embroidery of alienation and self-actualisation with his mid-range fashion trends for over thirty years. That really is very impressive, almost mythically so, I thought whilst gazing at the crowds who were now alarmingly tightly packed around me. I'm a slow getting what's really happening sort of gal. I need things more than spelled out. A huge, epic 19th century oil painting will usually do it, say Gericault's Raft of the Medusa. But what was becoming polycarbonate clear even to me now, was this: The fashionista gathered around me weren't all looking like early adopters keen to wear the latest trend. The fashionista hanging around Bill's final scene was a tribute to heterogeneity; the final stage of consumerism, the playing out of the individual. Hot pants, rave wear, fake fur, ripped, glam, jumpsuits, jodhpurs, sports luxe, platforms, capri, skinny, flares, punk, duster, rave, glam and hip… the list goes on. All competed in a glorious mismatch of decades, styles, patterns and fabrics and there wasn't a discernible trend in sight. Was Bill's 'let's all wear the same clothes,' business model defunct? Had it become, well old-fashioned? Had 'using clothes to express your imposed by structure identity,' lost its way. Or become so omni-platform that it's okay to say, 'I'm a postmodern anti-imperialist, capitalist, LGBT, gun holding, beef burger eating, vegan?'

Then I had a fashion retail epiphany. If individuality is in, what happens to poor billionaires who have based their empires on trends, the collective, the mass? How could Bill put an order in for that? Can you imagine it? The sweatshop wheels would literally stop turning every time one garment was made. Poor Bill, had he been hoist by his own petard? If the modernist fashion trend was dead, could Bill be losing money? If Bill was losing money, money, his one great love, his Wallis Simpson, what would that do to him? Could this explain his defeated and scared look when he saw me? Would this have been enough to make him jump off the balcony? Not murder but suicide. Should the police be looking for a note rather than a perpetrator?

I was so lost in thought that I bumped into Harvey and the Buyers without noticing. Fortunately for me, they were so intently discussing the plunge that they didn't notice my multi-faceted oddness.

'Look the teachers are going back into the building with the police,' Twinkle, Harvey's best friend shouted excitedly.

Harvey and his posse all looked over and said in sync, 'So which one did it, Maggie Twill or Cotton, Josue or Jonathan. Can you tell a killer by their clothes?'

'Yes, I'm sure you can,' they all agreed.

'Who was that TV box set psychopathic killer? Kind to children and small animals and only killed other psychopaths.' Harvey hissed malevolently.

'You mean the one where the main psychopath dressed casually but impeccably in chinos, the perfect T-shirt and a beautifully tailored jacket, all put together with laconic grace,' answered several of his followers as they slowly stitched something together.

'Yes,' replied Harvey who was clearly concocting a plan.

Then Harvey and his Buying coven all slowly turned their pretty blonde heads in the direction of Jonathan. They applied hot cherry lipstick and attitude as they contemplated their sumptuary deductions. Then Harvey said thoughtfully, 'Jonathan is wearing nice chinos.'

His coven said 'Yes' in unison.

'And Jonathan,' Harvey weaved, 'always wears the perfect T-shirt.'

'Yes, he does,' agreed the gang.

'And his perfectly tailored jacket always fits him with laconic grace, doesn't it?' Harvey added.

'Yes, it does,' the posse whispered thoughtfully.

Then Harvey said in, I suspect, a louder than intended whisper, 'I know who did it.'

All eyes turned to him, the staff, the police, the media, the homeless and me. Harvey was the centre of attention, a place he always craved. His starlight moment, he was silent for a nano-second and then blurted, 'I saw Jonathan on the balcony. I was walking into the Square and I looked up and Bill was falling and Jonathan was on the balcony smoking a cigarette.'

Harvey looked around wide-eyed and giddy with audience adoration. You could have heard a pin drop. He composed himself and theatrically breathed in. 'Jonathan must have pushed Bill Wonder off the balcony,' he gasped, swooning into Twinkle's consoling arms.

'Yes, I saw it too,' someone else called out.

'So did I,' said another.

'Yes, I did,' added another voice.

'Me too.'

'And me.'

Jonathan was a smoker and used the balcony regularly to have a sneaky fag; in fact he was out there most of the time. The students would open the window in the studio and shout out to him if they needed props or advice. Often he would put his sunglasses on and act like the world existed to entertain him and their requests were ignored. Most of the regulars in the square would have spotted Jonathan on the balcony at some point. He stood out as you turned in from Alfred Street. He looked rather like the hunchback of Notre Dame guarding his cathedral. Harvey's story was now being confirmed by several others. And I could just see the headlines, 'Ethereal Blond Midwich Buyer sees the killer. Others confirm the story is true.' Jonathon had been unstitched, good and proper.

Jonathan, unaware of his fate, had flounced back into the school and was waiting by the lifts but the detective was standing at the main entrance and had heard it all. I couldn't hear what was said but the huge glass windows served well as an amphitheatre and we, the audience, watched as the arrest unfolded.

Jonathan is very tall and the detective was rather small and Jonathan was wearing his super noise blocking headphones, he didn't appear to notice the detective when he spoke to him. Mags Twill who was now standing next to Jonathan and could see and no doubt hear the policemen, pointed at Jonathan in a 'look behind you' way and signed 'take your headphones off.' Jonathan ignored her. Mags Twill did some more semaphoring and Jonathan finally reluctantly pulled his head phones off and rolled his baby blues. The handcuffs slipped on and Jonathan was steered to one side. After a moment's silence whilst Jonathan processed what was happening, he dropped to the floor and let out a loud piercing wail. After the scream Jonathan cried, cried like a large loud baby, his sobs became uncontrollable keening. I suspect the detective was used to proper criminals. Hard men who never cry and would be indignant, defiant types, who would say things like, 'You got the wrong bloke, you're having a laugh, my solicitor will have you for this.' Uncontrollable, hysterical crying from a 6 ft 4 man must have been disconcerting and, well, a bit girly.

I looked around and noticed that several people were filming the arrest on their phones.

Jonathan, in a "trying not to get noticed" attempt, had wrapped a Pucci copy chiffon scarf around his sodden miserable face and snot ridden Maraschino jacket. The detective must have decided that a tall, handcuffed and sobbing creature wearing a brightly patterned head scarf, really would be too much for the crowd and he must have asked if there was a back door. The boys in blue led the man wrapped in purple, red and yellow to the back door which opened by the industrial bins where I was now hiding.

Jonathan, in between sobs choked out, 'But I was with Trixie. She was in the lift with me. Ask her, I couldn't have done it.'

As the door opened, I turned and my slow reflexes could have been my undoing as Jonathon stared straight at me. But rather than shout, 'Look, it's her. Why is she here? If anyone's guilty, it's her not me.' He said nothing and just looked even more desperate, confused and sad.

I knew that Jonathan believed in sartorial signs and symbols and I guess my 1959 Chanel Comeback tweed suite bricolage with accessories from Clockwork Orange smeared with blood and feathers must have been the final cultural and symbolic contumely for Jonathan. He looked straight through me and collapsed into the waiting police car and dropped his head into his lap.

Chapter 5
Shopping or Fanaticism

The party broke up soon after Jonathan's arrest and I finally for Oxford Street. I couldn't believe that Jonathan had been collared for the murder of Bill. Jonathan was so witty and urbane and well, rather critical and verbally malicious, but I would never have thought he was a killer. Was it a coincidence that he had picked the exact moment that I had gone back to school with my accidental purloined booty, to push Bill off the balcony? It was surprising that Jonathan had the time to approach Bill, presumably in the few seconds he was in the staffroom alone whilst I was hiding in the plant room and then ran back into the office when I opened the door. Unless of course he didn't do it and actually it now occurred to me, that if that was the case, I was Jonathan's alibi. Was I the only person who could verify the almost impossible timings of his funambulist fate?

'Can I help Jonathan without incriminating myself?' I mused and then a darker thought occurred. 'If they think Jonathan killed Bill, they won't be looking for anyone else.'

I was so lost in thought that I didn't notice Trixie Woo the fashion design lecturer speaking to me.

'Sadie, Sadie, are you okay, why are you wearing such a strange outfit?' she said.

Trixie was wearing a strange outfit herself, an American football outfit with helmet, shoulder pads and a toboggan. She was also eating a huge pink candy floss. I wondered whether Jonathon's trenchant advice about how she should never wear calf length skirts because of her cankles and broad but diminutive height had finally completely undone her clothing aesthetic.

'Trixie,' I cried, 'have you heard the news?'

'Of course I have,' she said in an abstract way.

'About Bill?'

Trixie eyed me uncertainly then said in a hushed voice, 'Sadie. Don't tell anyone but I rang in sick today, I'm going to the opening of NFFW.'

And then I remembered the other paradigmatic fashion shifting event that was happening today. The other event, the planned event was the opening of the new fashion shop NFFW with the launch of its new haute couture trickle-down mid-range mash up collection called Pepto.

NFFW was owned by Bill's nemesis "Carlo Monte Carlo", a Spanish businessman who was rapidly taking over the fast fashion world and Bill had tried everything in his power to block NFFW opening on Oxford Street. Important people in government were canvassed, planning objections were raised. When NFFW won, rumour had it that Bill even tried old-fashioned fisticuffs having waited for Carlo Monte Carlo's limo to pull up, Bill opened the door and said, 'Get the fuck out of my street' whilst rolling his shirtsleeves up in preparation for a fight. I personally admire this approach the best.

NFFW uses a different manufacturing model to Bill; it has its own sort of okay sweatshops in Europe, unlike Bill who always contracted out to India or Bangladesh. NFFW'S business model which uses fussy European workers who expect basic human rights such as toilets and buildings that don't fall down would initially appear counterintuitive if you're a profit hungry master of the universe. However, because NFFW owns their clothes factory and they are in Europe they can respond more quickly to the ever more rapid fashion cycle. NFFW had quickly realised that the discourse of fashion is obsolescence. Stylistic change is the driver of fast fashion and deceleration is the enemy. To this end NFFW had designed factories so quick to respond to a new trend that they could now produce clothes within minutes of them being cat walked down the runway. This had made them the darlings of the high street and the web ocean.

Their clothes were more expensive than Bill's but that didn't seem to bother the customer. It was being the first to purchase that was all important. Bill's fast fashion was old school in comparison. 3rd world sweatshops and as cheap as possible meant that trends could not be turned around at the drop of a pin. Patterns had to be sent out to India, designers and garment technologists had to be flown in. Discussions had, cultural misunderstandings dispelled. This all took forever and then even if the decaying exploitative factories could produce garments quickly, the clothes then had to be shipped back to the UK. Bill's fast fashion shops simply could not keep up with the rapid rate of change at NFFW.

But now in a very odd coincidental way, roughly an hour after Bill's demise, the launch of the new NFFW fashion shop on Oxford Street was about to happen. I considered the possibility that the two events might be linked in some way. Did Carlo Monte Carlo pay someone to kill Bill just before he unveiled his fashion launch? Probably not, I reasoned, given that Bill's death would probably win the publicity rating. In which case could Bill have jumped just to spite him? Maybe Bill wasn't murdered; maybe it was the sheer discordance of their huge egos clashing on the same day which meant one was destined to fall. And let's face it, Bill was old, nearly 90, probably too old to still be playing world domination games. I wondered if billionaires have some sort of Alpha demigod club, where ordinary life has become so mundane that they play ridiculously high-stakes Russian roulette for entertainment. Oxford Street would be a fiefdom worth fighting for.

NFFW had been clever on many levels; it had run an internet marketing campaign using all the new social media platforms, Sinkypics, Mongrel, Wavyhair to name a few. The campaign continually twittered and snapchatted about the exclusivity of the new Pepto range, how only 10,000 garments would be available at the new Oxford street store from 10 am on that fashion full June day. It implied that the Pepto range was costly because it was haute couture, hand stitched in a Parisian atelier, designed by Umo Betrolli just before he choked on a fishbone and died. Worn by Matilda Ellipse the new pop diva when she recorded her hit, 'I'm so rich I spend money all the time.' They were clothes never to be bought again, mass-produced one-off originals, and they were beyond exciting. Obscene amounts of money had been spent on the opening launch and I began to think that Bill may have had a stroke or heart attack from the sheer audacity of it all. Bill was the most competitive entity I have ever hurried past, head bent in servitude. He would not have taken this well. It highlighted his stores shortcuts, it made him seem old-fashioned, an anachronism. A bit like the sailing ship in Turner's Fighting Temeraire, being pulled to its last berth by the quicker more efficient European steam boat.

'What happened to Bill?' Trixie cut in.

'He's dead.'

'He was old,' she replied matter-of-factly.

I thought about the name of the new range, Pepto. Pepto was a shocking pink and of course Bill's 'Wonder' girdle was allegedly a shocking pink. It was one of the first undergarments to be made using a new synthetic pink dye. Was the choice of colour deliberately antagonising? A pink flag to a retail red bull?

'Do you think they're all going to the NFFW launch as well?' I asked pointing to a crowd of women dressed in stilettos and office wear also eating candy floss

'Yes, everyone eating Candy floss is going to the launch.'

'Really.'

'When you signed up with your credit card details it said you had to eat at least one candyfloss.'

'Why?'

'It all forms part of a living art installation event. It's not just a fashion event Sadie, we the ordinary people are all part of the process.'

'By eating candy floss?'

'Yes and buying the clothes of course.'

'Of course,' I agreed

My mobile rang and as I rummaged around in my 'I'm not a shopping bag' bag Trixie helpfully held it open for me.

'Is it true; is it true, Sadie, what they're saying? Did you kill him?' It was Bubbe.

'I'm not sure,' I replied as Trixie and I were becoming more densely packed in the crowd of strangely over excited women.

'What you don't know? If he's dead or if you killed him?'

'Bill Wonder is definitely dead,' I confirmed in a distracted way as an odd mesmerising sound like a repetitive high-pitched trill filled Oxford street and I had a wild and uncontrollable urge to buy an NFFW dress. 'I am an early adopter,' I shouted uncontrollably.

'What, what are you saying? You don't know if you killed someone? What it is with you youngsters, in my day it was pretty clear,' Bubbe was saying but I wasn't really listening as I was becoming more and more concerned about the people around me who were flailing their arms and legs around as if trying to suppress uncontrollable urges.

'Trixie what's happening to them?' I asked.

Trixie and I were now being jostled along by the crowd of women dressed in stilettos and office wear and the crowd were now making high pitched banshee sounds and sort of sniffing the air raptor-like. They were also chanting a rhythmic zombie "peep toe, peep toe".

'What, who's Trixie?' Bubbe was saying on the phone.

'Well, I definitely didn't actually kill him,' I said very loudly in case Bubbe could be overheard, 'but I might have had something to do with it.' I whispered.

'Good girl,' Bubbe said proudly.

And Bubbe said, 'Moon, I have to go, if I don't take the meds at the right time, they poison the food.'

'What fresh hell of shopping fetishism am I witnessing now?' I muttered to the dead phone line.

A pink open topped Cadillac stopped by a pink carpet and several male dancers wearing pink thongs and nipple stubs got out of the car. One of the dancers opened the car door and Rafonda, the sister of Umo Betrolli exited wearing a Pepto pink girdle which looked exactly like the Wonder corset illustrations. Balanced precariously on Rafonda's shoulders was a haute couture Pepto pink leather coat with studded silver stars. Thigh high pink leather stiletto boots and a sparkling diamanté necklace finished off the ensemble. The outfit complemented the pink highlights in her platinum extensions and she glistened like a damp marshmallow grown up power puff girl.

'Sadie, look at Rafonda. She's a fully formed example of the underwear driven cliché, 'strong independent woman,' Trixie said whilst jumping up and down on the spot.

'This isn't a coincidence. Carlo Monte Carlo is probably gutted that Bill is no longer around to see it,' I said to Trixie.

'Yes. It's just like the Wonder girdle on the Dora Duffy mannequin outside Bill's new office,' she replied.

'Wait, what? Bill had a Dora Duffy mannequin dressed in a Wonder girdle outside his temporary office?'

'Yes, he brought his collection over from the old head office when he moved in.'

'Okay and…'

Trixie interrupted and said in a very supercharged, I've-forgotten-how-to-breathe way, 'Yes. There's an 1870's steam-moulded spoon busk crinolette reinforced with strips of whalebone, actual whalebone. And a wonderful long straight through shoulder to hem corset with multiple garter harnesses and a flirty thirties Betty Boop with curvy waistline and built in brassiere and a forties Firmfit…'

'But what about the Wonder girdle?' I shouted.

'Look at Rafonda's accessories,' Trixie said in a jittery way. 'She's wearing a Pepto pink leather coat with studded silver stars. And look Sadie; look at her thigh high pink leather stiletto boots. And fake diamanté necklace.'

'I guess she doesn't look bad for a 72-year-old. But I'm very interested in the Wonder Girdle outside…' I replied but Trixie was no longer by my side she was pushing herself to the front of the crowd of fashionistas who were now banging on the window of NFFW. At that moment the pink shop blinds rolled up to reveal a window display of candy floss stalls festooned with pink lanterns and bunting shaped like washing lines with cut-out Pepto pink girdles fluttering ominously. This was clearly too much for the crowd's rampant commodity fetishism and the feral shoppers gathered around me started to round on Rafonda. They moved slowly, probably because they were dressed in less than appropriate militant wear but it was obvious their intention was to surround Rafonda and rip the clothes off her back. Rafonda's expressionless botoxed face contorted into a spasm of neck muscle and eye twitching. She was bravely shielded by her dance troupe. Their bare chests were bearing the brunt of the shellac claws. As two of the dancers fell, a hero appeared wearing an American football outfit with helmet, shoulder pads and a toboggan. He or she was clearing a path for Rafonda and dancers with a hockey stick. Fortunately, this gave the nimble dancers just enough time to get through a hastily erected barricade before the shoppers stampeded into the new shop.

I was starting to back away but realised I was no longer holding my shopping bag, which apart from useful things like keys and credit cards also held Bill's family album. Had it been stolen? No, I remembered Trixie was holding it. I had no choice but to follow her into the shop. At least she was very easy to spot in her American football outfit. The shop was now swarming with deranged fashionistas who were viciously shoving and shouldering each other aside to tear clothes from the gondolas. Some frenzied fashionistas held upholstery guns and were firing at will. Older fashion tribes armed with knitting needles cross stitched their way through the shop, jabbing the eyes of shoppers who got in their way. They showed no mercy and simply stepped on the fallen with sharp stiletto shoes. I saw Trixie sliding under the gondolas in her toboggan collecting garments that had fallen to the floor. She was laughing in a frenzied way.

'Trixie!' I called out. 'I need my bag.'

Trixie replied, 'Today I will win.'

'Okay but can I have my bag? It's on your shoulder,' I replied.

'I am small but nimble and not suffering from sleep deprivation or sugar induced fatness,' she said with a wild triumphant look.

I picked up a pink trickle-down dress. A frenzied fashionista made a grab for it but I gave her a fierce growl and she backed away, obviously my Clockwork Orange ensemble still swayed some power.

'Trixie,' I coaxed, 'look what I've got.' I said shamelessly flaunting the cheap pink polyester dress.

Trixie nervously came towards me. She was shaking and hyperventilating as she reached out to snatch it.

I pulled it back and said curtly, 'No, first give me my bag.'

Trixie looked confused. I pointed to her shoulder. She looked surprised. I offered her the dress and quickly slid my bag off her shoulder. I think she may have nodded in some sort of recognition as I backed away but I wasn't sure and then some crazed fashionistas pushed over one of the candy floss stalls and cheered as a weird chemical candy floss glop seeped across the floor and several fashionista bent down and started to lick it up.

'It's a military grade hallucinogenic,' a passing crazy eyed fashionista assured me.

'Trixie, do you want to come home with me?' I said to Trixie who was now ripping feathery pink garments off a mannequin display and shaking her head backwards and forwards uncontrollably.

I guessed not.

I backed out of the shop avoiding fashionistas who were now on their knees retching up thick pink fibrous candy floss puke and then ducked underneath an upended lamp post which several fashionistas were using to batter their way into the stockroom. When I made it outside a sub group had climbed up on the Belisha beacons and were throwing lighted hair lacquer cans at the shop window. They were holding a flag and had written in I think blood the words "I shop therefore I am".

'I have to say the last few hours had been pretty full on even for London.' I sighed as I walked away.

As I strolled down Oxford Street I had an uneasy feeling I was being followed. I looked around and to the sides but couldn't see anyone but I sensed a trail. I walked faster and the uneasy feeling sped up. I slowed but the shadow of surveillance still loomed. I walked for some time and then exhausted I stopped for something to eat at a cafe. *First things first*, I thought as I took the worn leather album out of my bag and flopped down in a chair. I was just about to finally open it when I heard

'Sadie, Sadie is that you, what's gone wrong with your foundation today?' It was Kimberley Clark, an ex-fashion merchandising student.

Kimberley wasn't liked by the other students. She was a little too blunt but her fashion forecasting was always bang on the button. Her dress sense was very 1980s power dressing; high neck blouses, wide lapels and big shoulders. Today she was wearing an eighties charcoal grey three piece Armani suit and was oozing professional authority.

'Sadie,' she enthused excitedly, 'no bombs today?'

The waitress looked alarmed and Kimberley laughed, 'The last time I saw you Sadie, I was helping you lead students out the emergency exit because there was a bomb scare. Do you remember? It was a false alarm.' She added to the waitress.

'Oh yes,' I laughed. 'It was a suitcase full of cheap clothes.'

'But the bomb disposal team were hot.'

'Although I am not sure that their padded clothes would have actually stopped them from being blown up.'

'Fearlessly brave as well,' she giggled in a raucous way

'Are you still working as a merchandiser at Compton's?' I asked.

Kimberley sniggered,

'You mean the job I got by using a mixture of cunning stunts and sly tactics?'

I raised an eyebrow.

'You were so mad at me when I stitched Adonia up.'

'Well you didn't play fair, you told Compton's she already had a job offer from Best Girl.'

'All's fair in career advancement. Anyway I quit last year.'

'Why?'

'Mmmm, I'm not sure. Could it be the institutional nature of shop work? Or the long hours for poor pay? Or even the unequal distribution of work and reward, like I worked really hard so that shareholders can get rich.'

'What do you do now?' I asked tactfully whilst secretly being impressed that Kimberley had seen through the hegemonic order of capitalism so quickly.

'I left last year to set up my own business.'

'What, in fashion?'

'I run my own business now called CORMUF.'

'Actually I read about you somewhere. What does the abbreviation stand for?'

'Charge Older Rich Men for Sex to Pay for your University Fees.'

'That's it. Your USP is prostitution without exploitation.'

'Probably? I'm doing really well. Everyone who works for me has to be a genuine student and has to pass all sorts of IQ tests and health and counselling screenings. We also screen clients, get rid of the pervs and paeds.'

'Oh yes that's what I was reading. Your checks are so rigid and require such a high level of "within social norm" screening, that professional people who have passed include them in their work CVs.'

'Yep, that's right. I'm making more money out of the screening than the prostitution nowadays. But what's this?' Kimberley said picking up the album and opening it before I could protest. 'Sadie. It's full of photographs of topless young men, like geeky, unassuming young men. Maybe they could be hot in a beta way, it's quite fashionable now.'

I made a grab for the book.

Kimberley pulled it away. 'Sadie, are you venturing into my line of business? Note to self we use the internet now.'

I wrestled the album back from Kimberley. She was right the book was full of black and white photographs of young men. They had been photographed side on and front and most of them had very terrible postures, some even had pigeon chests or pectus issues. *How curious*, I thought.

'There isn't a hint of porn or exotica about them,' I replied indignantly. 'They look almost medical or scientific and look, under each photograph there's a serial number.'

'That's a young Hayat Miyake,' Kimberley said. 'I recognise his profile. I spent a long time lusting after him at my graduation ceremony. Isn't he even richer than Bill?'

'Yes he's much richer,' I agreed, 'and he was wearing a really nice suit.'

'Mongolian yak wool, it's the rarest type of wool in the world. Only 40 garments are made a year. Is that a young Tom Strip, the sportswear billionaire, he was a really fat kid,' Kimberley said, pointing to another photograph.

'Yes I think it is,' I agreed. 'And I think that's the young Ken Huddle, the education minister.'

'He hasn't changed much,' Kimberley added.

'Sadie, why have you got a rather dry collection of photographs of young men?'

'It's Bill's.' I said in an unguarded moment.

'Bill's! Was he running some sort of escort agency, in his day?'

'What?'

'I mean who was his marketing advisor?'

'I don't know,' I said whilst leafing through the album. Could the album be photographs of Bill's friends? Did he say to them, hey why don't you come over and take your tops off and then sit or stand very still while I take photographs of your chests? Could they be his lovers, his harem of rather plain young men photographed in such a non-descriptive way to enhance the pleasure in a kitchen sink realism sort of way? If so, could the extravagance of being a billionaire led to a strange puritan desire for the absolute ordinary? No, it didn't make sense, not if his taste in women was anything to go by.

'Sadie, do you want a face cleanser to take the weird makeup off?' Kimberley asked whilst waving one at me.

'Why have I been suspended for taking this?' I said indignantly.

'What you've been suspended?' Kimberley gasped .

I looked at Kimberley, should I tell her, probably not the whole story, not yet. 'Yes for taking this album, accidentally taking the album that is,' I replied.

'Really and you don't know why.'

'No idea, this is the first time I've looked through it. I thought I'd understand when I opened it.'

'Did you piss Gita from HR off? She was very officious and scary.'

'I don't think so,' I replied hesitantly.

'Come on Sadie there has to be more to this,' Kimberley said, turning the album upside down and giving it a firm shake.

Something dropped to the floor. Kimberley picked it up. 'It's a very old photograph; there's two women. Wait Utility clothing post war, rationing, Board of Trade. The tall woman is wearing a CC41 grey jacket with square shoulders, 3 statutory buttons and no pockets. Pretty sure her matching skirt is exactly 19 inches. See I did listen to your lectures.'

I nodded impressed.

Her tiny friend with the weird face is wearing overalls, a turban and heavy wedge shoes. They're standing in a grimy back yard of some sort of factory. There's a sign that says, 'Silver's lingerie workshop'.

I snatched the photograph off Kimberley. The smaller woman smiled at the camera; eyes screwed up to avoid the gritty sun. Her resolute glare was very familiar. If I added wrinkles and a little sag, her resemblance to my Bubbe was uncanny and there was no mistaking the name of the sweatshop. This was my grandmother's lingerie workshop in Hackney Downs. The factory she would regale as we made cinnamon balls in her turquoise Formica kitchen when I was a child, as she explained the cut, make and trim of transitional nether region undergarments.

I cast a searching eye over this young Bubbe in Bill Wonder's family album.

'What does this all mean?' I asked the young Bubbe in the photograph.

She looked at me squarely back and seemed to say, 'Surely at last, you see what the nogoodnik did.'

Bubbe had warned me about Wonder and now her warning didn't seem like the circuitous ramblings of a confused geriatric. Bubbe and Wonder had history. The warning had a context. Whatever had happened Bubbe was too scared to ever speak about it. I had a visceral feeling of the wrongness of this. My Bubbe was as feisty as fuck. She wouldn't have gone down without a fight and even if she did have to acquiesce to the power of the multinational, why keep it a secret, why take it to the grave? She would have discussed this with me. She happily spoke about far more controversial issues. My Bubbe spoke about everything toilet habits, sex, money and style but this she kept tightly sealed, coffin tight. Presumably it had something to do with my grandmother's small independent lingerie workshop and the billionaire clothing giant Bill Wonder.

It didn't make any sense, I know she would have sat me down and said, 'So child, let me tell you about greedy bloodsucking multinationals.'

Whatever had happened it looked like Bill had trussed her up good and proper.

'Don't worry Bubbe,' I said to her photographic image. 'I'll discover what Wonder did and hopefully expose him for the nogoodnick gonef he undoubtedly is, well was.'

Chapter 6
Twisted Tailoring

I slept in and was awoken by the postman wedging a letter through my rather small letter box. I felt a dart of excitement as I opened the handwritten envelope; the only letters I usually receive are bills or circulars. Inside I found a white card and the words 'Mr Dapplewhite requests your company for afternoon tea on the 27th June at 2 pm, in The Basement, Dapplewhites, Oxford Street, London W1. *What a curious development*, I thought whilst dropping the envelope into my fake designer tool box. Why did Mr Dapplewhite want to see me and how does he know where I live?

I had decided to visit my grandmother at her nursing home in Bournemouth and try and get the story out of her. I got up early and put on a pair of jeans and sweatshirt, packed up the photograph album as a visual aid and booked the train from Paddington. Whilst eating three rice cakes I turned on terrestrial TV and caught the last few seconds of a report about Bill's death followed by an interview with Judith Trouser, my old university lecturer and the leading authority on fashion fantasies and subliminal messages. I had just finished reading her new book, '1974 whatever happened to James Vicary.'

Judith Trouser was saying, 'Shopping as we saw this morning can be contradictory in that it is an experience that both yields pleasure and anxiety. Shopping is a delightful experience that can quickly become a "nightmare", for there is a dark, as well as a light side to shopping. The desire and the curbing of desire which shopping entails, is the point at which the tensions and the premises of modernity and postmodernity are perhaps most apparent.'

'Thank you Judith,' said a slightly bemused news reporter, 'and now let us take you back to the disturbing scenes of yesterday morning.'

A dazed reporter was standing outside the closed and boarded up new NFFW shop on the corner of Berry Street. 'One death and 24 casualties have been reported so far in the most frenzied shopping launch yet. Safety rules on shopping will now have to be re-written. We are now turning to our live on scene expert retail reporter Jessy Spender.'

'Thank you, James. Yes, this has been a shocking day. As it got closer to the 10 am launch, the NFFW marketing department must have been worried they had overplayed the hype. Oxford street was packed full of thousands of fashionistas who hadn't slept all night and were displaying frenzied uncontrollable urges. The fashionistas started to bang on the metal shutters and shop workers started to panic. I am now going to cut to Phil Henderson, the store manager.'

Phil was clearly in shock, 'We were not prepared for the onslaught,' he trembled. 'We begged them to stop banging on the shutter but they took no notice, we were very scared. Most of the zero-contract staff fled, leaving only a handful of permanent staff and most of them were hiding. Houp Emiloi was a brave man. He tried to stop the stampede but stood no chance. They just tore through him; he died in my arms.' Phil broke down and moved towards Jessy looking for human compassion.

Jessy looked mildly repulsed before composing herself, 'Thank you, Phil, yes it has been a truly shocking day. Now let's speak to Eddie Path, leading expert on mass hysteria,

Celebrity endorsement, marketing hype, sleep deprivation and as yet unidentified neuro stimulants, made the crowd's commodity fetishism uncontrollable. We can't really blame them for this behaviour and they shouldn't be punished for this addiction. The desire to be the first to purchase one of NFFW polyester copies of the Haute Couture designer outfit, retailing at 25% more than their usual pricing was just too much for them. Counselling and anti-retail therapy is recommended now.'

'Thank you, Eddie,' said the news reporter, 'we have one more interview with a survivor before we cut to the football results.'

The report cut to Trixie Wu, 'I sought advice from experts in the fashion frenzy field beforehand.' She laughed faltering, 'I used my toboggan to slide under the gondolas and collect garments that had fallen to the floor.' Trixie was now contorting with adrenalin, 'I was brave. This paid off. I picked up five faux leather dresses and a pink coat as I whizzed through the crowd. I think the candy floss liquid helped me slide. Then I had to get out. I stuffed the clothes down my undercarriage, put my head down and ran to the exit doors. Crazy stupid fashionistas were rampaging but American footballers don't usually buy ladies' fast fashion dresses, so I made it home and put it all on eBay, £5,000 per dress and £10,000 for the coat. It sold in seconds. I should have asked for more,' she finished breathlessly.

'Sorry, er, how much did you make?' asked the suddenly very interested reporter.

I signed in at Bubbe's nursing home and one of the nurses cheerily said, 'Another visitor for Bobena today, what a lucky lady.'

Bubbe was sitting up in her chair when I went into her room and said, 'Mein Gott Sadie, why do you look like Rosie the Riveter, are you a lesbian now?' before falling into a trance-like slumber.

'Bubbe, wake up,' I said whilst prodding her.

'Sadie, Sadie,' she muttered anxiously.

'Yes, I'm here Bubbe.'

'Sadie, do you know the English have their own language now?' she muttered.

'Bubbe, are you awake?'

'My granddaughter, Sadie, works for the hubris Wonder as a teacher you know, she is such a klutz of a girl,' she replied, her eyes tightly shut.

It was obvious Bubbe was having one of her days. A day when the toll of old age and the vast and complex medication she required to keep her alive, didn't mix well. I wondered whether she had been compos mentis for her first visitors. I sat on her bed unsure what to do next. I'm always rather scared about leaving her room and mixing with the other old people. They were so needy and desperate and you always have to check the chairs for unsavoury stains before you sit down. Once I had inadvertently let a very polite and well-dressed elderly woman out of the front door because she had said (very convincingly), that she couldn't reach the top bolt. This had caused a nursing home lock down and a police search.

So instead, I sat and chewed at my nails and willed her to wake up. Bubbe had a line of photographs on her window sill; I had looked at most of them before and never tired of her telling me about the people in them. I picked up a photograph of Bubbe and her best friend Anai Foucaitt. Anai Foucaitt was a legendary person who I had sadly never met, but would have loved to. She was a conceptual artist and one of the first female conceptual artists of this century. She had started building her art installations in the fifties when most women were being forced back into the home after the war. Her early work integrated ordinary household items such as kettles and stockings, with giant spiders and often huge penises. Then she went onto her womb stage and then gruesome murders of women in a very Freudian, psychotherapy way. Her work was both disturbing and revealing and very much ahead of its time. I was unsure if she was still alive and attempted to google her but I didn't have Wi-Fi and the nursing home was charging 97p a second to use theirs.

In the photograph, the ladies were sitting pretty and chatting on the deck of an ocean liner, the QE2 I think. They were lounging on stripy deck chairs wearing pink and blue "Have mercy" wiggle dresses and confetti straw hats, watching men play shuffleboard on deck. Bubbe had told me that she and Anai had gone to New York on a buying trip, maybe even a holiday, but she would never admit to that. Bubbe thought holidays were a waste of money. Anai was working on an assemblage of a partly dressed woman sitting on a grassy knoll, eating a pastrami on rye, viewed through the shutter slats of a window in a closed Parisian millinery shop and needed a New York deli sandwich to complete the piece. Bubbe had said she had some unfinished business in New York but then swiftly changed the subject and told me about the disgusting cheesecake they had dared to serve her in the deli.

As I sat down and scrutinised how the ravages of age played out of Bubbe's face I realised she was holding a letter. I carefully extracted it from her rheumy grip. The envelope said 'Delivered by hand' and was dated today so presumably her last visitor had given it to her. I opened it, Dear Bobena, we tried to get the book but someone else took it moments before us. I'm assuming whoever took it also killed SW. My employees did find these two photographs of the floor near a desk by the balcony. Fondest regards HM

The first photograph was of Bubbe and Anai standing outside Lackeys, the New York department store, Bubbe was wearing a tight knitted lilac wool Givenchy twinset with a black beret. Anai was dressed in a black Balenciaga sack dress and they were having a heated argument. The setting was cleverly incongruous and looked staged in a Cecil Beaton way with my grandmother perhaps playing Audrey Hepburn and Anai, Marilyn Monroe.

In the next photograph, Bubbe and Anai were on the ground brawling and Anai's Balenciaga sack dress had ridden right up. I guess that type of unstructured style will do that if you're brawling (I wasn't sure and in many ways didn't really even want to dwell on it), but there was something a bit strange about Anai's undergarments. I guess a little too lumpy in certain places and not lumpy enough in others.

Bubbe groaned so I quickly wedged the letter back in her hand. This seemed to soothe her.

I prodded her again and said, 'Wake up; I want to ask you about Bill's photograph collection of weedy men. And now the two photographs of you and Anai fighting in New York'

'Always look at the vanishing point.' she replied somnolently.

Then I remembered I was wearing the Chanel two tone black and beige slingbacks. 'Look Bubbe, I've got an original pair of Chanel shoes,' I said enthusiastically whilst holding them under her nose. This still did not wake her and I resigned myself to accepting that nothing would today, so I packed up my stuff and left a note that said "Dear Bubbe, I visited whilst you were asleep, call me".

I took the train back to London.

I didn't want to fixate on Anai Foucaitt's undercarriage but there was something about it that didn't look right. Also who was SW and for that matter HM and was the letter referring to another book and murder that my grandmother was somehow involved in, or was it Bill Wonders death and therefore me. Everything about the last few days wasn't really adding up. Or maybe it was but I was a bit too involved in the action to actually see the pattern. I sighed in a desperate way and looked at the young man sitting across from them. There was something familiar about the theme song from the film he was watching on his phone.

'Are you watching The Naked Corset?' I asked

'Yes I'm, checking for subliminal messages,' he replied.

'When I analysed it on a purely denotative level, I was drawn to Dora's husband. He was remarkably handsome and sad and looked like a poster boy for Prozac until he went on the revenge killing spree. Then he's decidedly chipper and well, even hotter,' I said.

'Yes, well there certainly more to it than that,' he said, clearly un-impressed with my analytical skills.

'Yes, of course there is, but I will take it as a sign,' I replied chirpily as it had suddenly become clear to me what my next move should be.

Chapter 7
Tribes

As I arrived at the backdoor, Josue was discussing the Jonathan situation with Laimdota the cleaner, 'He's been charged and sent to a remand prison in Bedford.'

Poor Jonathan, I thought, talk about, *Et tu Brute.* Jonathan was usually so popular, so worldly and urbane, and so well-liked by young fashionistas.

'Jonathan said he was in the lift talking to Trixie. But when they questioned her, she said no,' Josue added whilst powering up the steam cleaner.

'Well, he's kaput then,' Laimdota replied.

'Yes, I suppose he is,' Josue sighed whilst unleashing the steaming beast.

As the sound of the steam cleaner became more distant I made a dash for the tradesman's lift unlocked it and pressed floor three. But the lift didn't deposit me outside Bill's new office. It went straight up to the eighth floor. I tried again but it went straight down to the ground. After a few more goes it dawned on me that my lift key clearly wasn't an open all access type of key, more of a rather top or bottom one and so I plumped for the eighth floor.

I arranged myself in the plant room with a sandwich and a flask of tea and opened the door so that it was slightly ajar. I had collected a pile of backdated Haute magazines to read in case there was a lull in the snooping. As I peeped into the staffroom, it was obvious that the absence of Jonathan had changed the dynamics of the department. He was the influencer in our little troupe, we all wanted to be his friend, liked what he liked and hated what he hated. He was after all a tastemaker and we were all fag-hags. We all accepted that Jonathan was the king of the staffroom and his highly developed self-aesthetics, dictated who was in the "in-crowd" and who was too ugly, stupid or dull to be allowed access. Without Jonathan, the staff had lost their taste anchor and ghastly outfits were foot pedalling out of control. Maggie Cotton was wearing a mini skirt with drive in movie motifs that rather unfortunately had the wording, "enter here" with an arrow pointing in between her legs. Tanya, now free of Bill and Jonathan and presumably giddy with relief, had gone all secretary designer label and wore an outfit with so many abbreviations it was a bit like watching Sesame Street. Trixie, perhaps in protest, had chosen a lavish Elsa Schiaparelli evening gown but Jonathan may have been right on this, as she looked more like a hobbit than a glamour puss. Things were not looking good but I think the dull, ugly, stupid members of staff were all a bit relieved.

Alistair was telling Mags Twill, Alice and Maggie Cotton about visiting Jonathan. 'Tanya happily agreed to let me go; she's in a very good mood recently. She even giggled.'

I worried for Tanya; did she really think she had gotten off so lightly? Some other power-hungry control freak would be along soon and the people Bill surrounded himself with made him seem nice. Bill's squadron contained women whose balls were so big they couldn't cross their legs; I believe it's called chutzpah. The biggest baller was Sharleen, and I could imagine her sharpening her pinking shears and zipping up her sadism boots in preparation for the "where's my money" visit.

Maggie Cotton asked, 'Did Jonathan like the pin cushion in the shape of a duck?'

'The duck pin cushion was confiscated; the wardens just laughed and asked me if I was a friend of Dorothy's,' Alistair replied.

'Did you tone down your outfit?' quizzed Mags Twill.

'Yes,' replied Alistair. 'I wore my not so tight denim shorts and a plain blue crop top but realised I should have gone further. I had to walk through several doors and mesh wired stairs and prisoners and I'm pretty sure wardens shouted things like, butplugger, batty boy, chutney ferret, cock jockey and twink.'

'Oh dear, maybe jeans and a shirt next time,' said Mags Twill.

'Jonathan looked terrible, and looked old and kind of ugly. His hair has grown out and he can't ruffle it back into his textured modern quiff anymore and he sounded really desperate. He was crying and another prisoner shouted, "Everyone, it's happening again, get your phones out".'

'What's happening?' asked both Maggie's.

'A video of his arrest went viral. If he leaves his cell, crowds of inmates follow him around pretending to cry. They think it's hilarious but I think some are actually crying.'

'Poor Jonathan,' said Maggie Cotton.

'And he's talking like a farm boy in a sorta, "I be" accent, like those stupid but kind-hearted hairy characters from children's books about magicians and middle earth.'

'Why?' chorused everyone.

'I asked him, he said there were different tribes in prison and a gay tastemaker wasn't one, so he has decided to join the white working-class farm boy tribe before someone sticks a screwdriver up his arse,' explained Alistair.

The staff gasped.

'He did say he was surprised how quickly the Wiltshire farm boy he had buried 33 years ago came back.'

We all gasped. Jonathan came from a farm in Wiltshire, he didn't emerge fully formed from an eighties gay club.

'That doesn't sound good,' said Mags Twill, 'What is he doing?'

'Not much, sitting alone in his cell, he's sharing it with a man called Jed who also has an "I be" accent and a tattooed face and is in for a five-finger discount.'

'He sounds nice,' said Alice hopefully.

'He did start a conversation about tattoos and prison, he said tattoos can become a significant part of an inmate's uniform, not only marking the crime they're in for but serving as a way to communicate with others. Jonathan said if he wasn't so miserable and scared, he would find the visual iconography very interesting.'

'Yes, it really is,' gushed Alice. 'Do you know in Russia for instance, a tattoo of a dagger through the neck suggests that an inmate has murdered someone in prison and is available to carry out hits for others?'

'Umm, yes,' Maggie Cotton added, 'it is interesting how many fashion trends have bubbled up from prison uniforms.'

Suddenly, all the staff were engaged in a list of incarceration fashions; low hanging jeans, trainers without laces, sleeveless T-shirts, black and white stripes, the colour orange, jailhouse chic with gold stiletto heels, denim, prison blues, prison numbers.

Alistair was turning pink with disbelief and screeched, 'Ladies, ladies, please shut up. I was telling you about Jonathan in prison; it's not "let's discuss fashion flipping history". Jonathan needs our help, Jonathan, our Jonathan, the aesthete, the tastemaker, the cultural intermediary is struck in prison and he's really fucking scared, it's not a screenplay it's real. I'm deeply concerned about him. He seems broken; he's lost his swagger, his nonchalance, his confidence. He told me when he got out of the prison van, the prisoner sitting next to him said, "Come near me faggot and I will cut you," and I think the YouTube crying video has made things so much worse.'

The staff looked ashamed and Alistair continued, 'He thinks his life is ruined and I can't get what he did, as I left, out of my head.'

'What did he do?' gulped both Maggie's.

'He said please help me, please I beg you, get me out of here and then he grabbed my crop top and pulled it completely out of shape, it cost £580.'

Even I couldn't help a sharp intake of breath after that revelation which was a mistake as I inhaled dust which wedged itself in the right-hand corner of my mouth. As I flailed around trying not to sneeze, I had a profound sense of my ex-colleagues' unity and my loneliness. When I worked with them, I used to find them irritating and banal but now, now I am no longer "one of the gang", I think I am missing their camaraderie, well rivalry. As I made a grab for a surrogate handkerchief, I noticed a malnourished fairy peeking out from behind a clothes gondola and she appeared to be shaking her head in a disapproving way. I rubbed my eyes and when I looked again, she had gone. I ducked down to check if a slip mannequin had fallen behind the gondola but there was nothing there apart from a neatly folded package wrapped in muslin with a note that said, "Please open". As I undid the bow, I was mesmerised by the simple black cursive "Mila Schon". Could it be what I think it was? I thought as I excitedly pushed away the wrapping. I pulled out a white silk matelassé coat, with sequined collar and cuffs followed by a sleeveless sequined and beaded silver dress. Surely the simple but classic structure was unmistakable. It was a copy of the dress worn by Princess Lee Radziwill at the legendary black and white ball, held by Truman Capote to celebrate the launch of his non-fiction book, "In Cold Blood".

'My Bubbe will love this,' I gasped as I greedily added it to my tool kit along with my make-up and anti-bacterial hand wash. *As I'd been labelled a thief, I might as well act like one.*

I did a quick search of the plant room, could there be other designer classics wedged under boxes, screwed up out of sight? Nothing else of huge fashion importance leapt out but I did find a broken Manolo shoe. This was rather strange: Manolo's heels don't break; it was why they cost £6k a pair. They were guaranteed to withstand the heaviest of shopping expeditions. Even more curiously, someone had attempted to glue the transparent spindly heel back together. Who could have done that?

'I remember when I first met Jonathan. It was the eighties,' Mags Twill was nostalgically wittering when I got back to my spying position.

'Did you meet at the school?' Alice enquired.

'We were both headhunted by Bill but we first met at Dapplewhites.'

'Didn't Bill monopoly board all the falling boutiques in London around that time?' asked Maggie Cotton.

'Yes, he brought out Jane Shore, Samantha Jones and Bessie Blount and renamed them Best Girl. It was the Margaret Thatcher sell-out to multinationals decade,' Mags Twill replied.

'Loads of money decade,' laughed Maggie Cotton.

Mags Twill laughed gutsily. 'Wonder head office was the only place more ruthless than Dapplewhites back then. Any lack of confidence, any reflection on fairness, exploitation, ethics and you would be right out on your ear,' she chuckled in a blood lust way. 'Mrs Maud Wilson, Jonathan's aunty Maud, was head of merchandising at Dapplewhites. She had a razor-sharp head for a product, and not only a product but a product that would reflect the company's identity.' Mags Twill inhaled, 'She was a hard bitch but you had to admire her business acumen. What was her line "buy nothing unless you could make 87% profit, aim for 300%," what a lady. Would have given Thatcher a run for her money. Can't imagine what would have happened if they had met, the NHS and schools would have been privatised decades ago.'

'What happened to Aunt Maud?' asked Maggie Cotton.

'She died a few years ago,' Mags Twill replied. 'Jonathan was really upset but she did leave him that house in Ladbroke Grove, think it was valued at £4 million. Jonathan liked to imagine how they would portray her when they made the blockbuster film of his life. He decided she would stay exactly the same. The hip flask of gin in her Osprey handbag, purple rinse, neat twin sets, pearls and sensible leather shoes. He was going to give her a Mrs Slocombe edge, malapropisms and delusions of grandeur but then thought, "No, I will not stereotype a successful business woman as a pretentious fool because she no longer looks pretty." Although I don't think she ever did look pretty,' Mags Twill chuckled mischievously.

'Tell us the story of Jonathan's UM bag window again, his handbag de la resistance,' gushed Alice excitedly.

'Ah, the UM bag,' Mags Twill began. 'It was Dapplewhites' first attempt at tempting the new middle-classes to their shop.'

'Middle-class taste, tuh,' rasped Maggie Cotton, running her fingers through her tousled prickly blondie bob and leaving it to float upwards.

'The UM bag, what colour was it… Magnolia?'

'Pumpkin, we didn't have magnolia then,' corrected Maggie Cotton.

'You had one, didn't you?' laughed Alice.

'No, I bloody didn't,' said Maggie Cotton with such gusto that everyone stopped and stared, maybe she always wanted one.

'What was the marketing bumf? A white strap for the liberated woman who needs her hands free to work.' Mags Twill said.

'What about the white lining? How did it go? Something like… a soupcon of pathos, history and fashion classic, inspired by a convent school upbringing.'

'What utter bollocks?' Maggie Cotton retorted. 'Everyone knows that's purple.'

'What was the advertising slogan?'

All the staff chorused, 'A perfect weave for material happiness.'

And I couldn't help but laugh out loud.

'Did you just hear a noise coming from the plant room?' Maggie Cotton said.

'Yes, see it's the ghost,' Alice replied.

'Stop being ridiculous. I'll go and check, it's probably rats,' Mags Twill said.

Oh shit, I thought I can't get caught now I've got too much to do.

'What ridiculous self-obsessed quasi-religion trivia! Get the masses to desire a handbag that will stop them thinking about reality and war and exploitation,' exploded Joya the assistant principal in her usual angry righteous vegan way.

'Joya where have you been?' burst out Alice. 'Have you heard what happened?'

'Of course I have. I took some annual leave to help extract methane from Lake Kivi in the Democratic Republic of Congo. But I did have a mobile signal,'

Mags Twill hated Joya and would never let her steal the limelight, I realised I'd been spared for now.

Mags Twill powered on, completely ignoring Joya's arrival and continued her story.

'The Christmas window was the highlight of the year and Jonathan was so happy when he was asked to do the UM Bag display.'

'What did he do?' lisped wide eyed Alice.

'Jonathan placed the bag on a white cube in the middle of the window that he had also painted white, except it wasn't called white, it was called something like winter whisper. Dapplewhites sold out of UM bags 2 hours 37 seconds later, it was a record. Jonathan was a success; he was the new tastemaker of fashion retail that Christmas.'

Silence fell as everyone contemplated the tastefulness of Jonathan, and I flipped through a special for men edition of Haute. There was an interesting article about the great masculine renunciation which according to Haute had begun in the late 19th century when men gave up their claim to be considered beautiful and henceforth aimed at being only useful. Fortunately, I guess for fashion history the peacock male was now a growing phenomenon again and it's very on trend to re-eroticise the male body. How interesting, I mused whilst looking at men in chaps and unisex dresses.

On the next page was a list of this year's richest people in fashion. Bill was ranked fourth in the world. I am always interested in what makes a billionaire. Is it luck, inheritance, hard work, canny business abilities? Or is there a certain something else? I had read a report once that suggested there were certain life factors that lead people to become extraordinarily rich. One defining factor was a traumatic life event at the age of 11. I wondered if something traumatic had happened to Bill around this age. I guessed it might explain the total internet blackout of his past.

My musing about wealth was interrupted when Joya threw the latest copy of "Haute" on Alistair's desk and started to rant, 'This shit is full of white models that have their straight hair braided into cornrows, "cornrows" even the word annoys me.'

Alistair bravely or foolishly asked, 'Does it matter?'

It clearly did to Joya, she screeched, 'It's political, these images laugh in the face of racial divides, don't black women struggle enough in the hierarchy of traditional beauty?'

Alistair looked a bit confused, Joya growled, 'To put it more simply, black women aren't being hired as models but white models dressing up as black women are. It's racial fetishism, complete cultural appropriation.' Joya got up and did a sort of body performance as she spoke, 'Let's pull black beauty apart; look at their frizzy hair, let's do something with it, maybe their lips or bottoms next.'

Alistair continued his brave or foolish deflection, 'But lots of black women relax their hair – could that be called cultural appropriation of white beauty.'

Joya howled with frustration. 'Straightened hair is a necessity if you're a black woman,' she barked as she leant in towards Alistair and bellowed in his face. 'How do you think I got the management job here? Did I come to the interview with a 6-inch afro? Of course, I didn't. Do you think the American ex-president's wife could go around with an afro? Of course, she can't, no one would have voted for him.'

I would have loved to join in but appreciated that my fugitive hiding in the plant room status made me somewhat persona non grata. If I could have, I would have suggested there might be a problem with cultural-appropriation critiques, because they depend on reductive binaries, in this case "first-world" and "third-world" that preserve the hierarchical relations between the fashion industry and the cultures being appropriated. And instead of obsessing over whether certain forms of cultural appropriation are "good" or "bad", "racist" or "post-racial", we should ask what an "inappropriate" discourse is, and how can we move forward and challenge the idea of the absolute power and authority of Western fashion. But then again Joya was looking very angry and I might just have sat with my head down and buttoned my staircase lip.

Alistair was backing away now and to be fair, she was spitting as she spoke.

'There is even black politics involved in the names of braids: the Afro Caribbean British use the term "cane rows" because Caribbean slaves grow sugar cane; but the Americans call them "corn rows". And do you know what black people, who didn't have to suffer the indignity of slavery, call them?'

Alistair shook his head; he didn't look like he wanted to guess, fortunately it was a rhetorical question. 'They patriotically call them after their sovereign states: Senegalese twist, Ghana braids, Bantu knots, and yes, my Afro hair is not a fashion accessory or something to be parodied.'

Alistair said, 'Okay,' meekly.

Alistair's flaccid response seemed to anger Joya even more and as she looked around trying to find someone more interesting to engage with she glanced over at the plant room door which I was now peeking out of and very definitely locked eyes with me. She instantly stopped looking angry and instead looked curious.

Chapter 8
Structure or Agency

I wasn't entirely sure what would happen next, but I was aware that several metaphysical factors now came into play and I ran through the balance of probabilities as I backed towards the tradesman lift. Joya wasn't pretty enough for Jonathan's gang and was always a bit of an outsider that was good however she was the vice principal and would no doubt have so sort of duty to report me.

She was a fashion activist, a bit moral and human rightsy, "let's-be-kind-to-poor-people-in-3rd-world-countries" type of person. She was fond of saying, 'Fashion is based on the ideas, culture and economics of the west and made possible by the exploitation of the east.' Her motto went something like this. 'New York, Paris, London, social, culture and economic imperialism.' She certainly held non-conformist even radical views about the lovely pastel fashion industry and did tick quite a few, "I'm going to push the fat cat capitalist over the balcony" personality traits. This I hoped worked in my favour.

She was always very friendly with me particularly when she heard my surname. She would corner me in the staff room and say, 'So Sadie, I think you once told me your family owned a lingerie factory in Hackney, that's right, isn't it?' Or, 'So Sadie, it was lingerie your family made, wasn't it, corsets… is that right?' I tried to not engage in any conversations with her. I had only just got into Jonathan's gang myself and was only hanging on by a thread; I didn't want to blow my chances by befriending a shabbily dressed leftie loony. But she was unremitting and started buying me coffees that cost £12, and have a secret ingredient in them which tastes like lard.

In light of the family album exposé, I now began to think Joya had been on to something. Could Joya really be a clever activist even though she dressed so badly? Joya's outbursts coupled with her 'I do give a shit about injustice,' stance, really meant her days were numbered at the Wonder Fashion school but had she been working to a different agenda all along?

I almost got to the lift when the door opened and someone turned the fluorescent light strip on.

As the lights started to buzz Joya whispered, 'I'm alone. I'm coming in.'

'Okay,' I whispered back.

'What are you doing hiding in the plant room?' she said looking me up and down.

I was unable to formulate an answer and just stared back.

'Oh I see,' she said pointing to my fake toolkit with the Mila Schon hanging out of it. 'You're rooting through the plant room stealing seminal fashion garments before the schools closed down, aren't you?'

'Yes,' I replied relieved.

'Well then, I guess I'll just have to help you.'

'Really,' I gasped with relief.

'For sure I hate this fucking place. I resigned today,' Joya replied.

'What did you say?' I asked, starting to feel a rumbling of disparity myself.

'I said shove your stupid job. I'm going freelance.'

'Would you like some tea?' I asked her.

'Thanks,' Joya replied, taking the peace pipe, well flask.

'I'm sorry I was so rude and dismissive when you tried to make friends with me,' I said apologetically.

'Yes, you were. But I could see you were trying very hard to get into Jonathon's "we're so tasteful" gang,' she replied not unkindly.

'Yes, sorry about that. I did ignore you,' I replied sheepishly.

'Sadie, honey you do know you were never going to get into Jonathon's clique don't you.'

'Really, I thought I was almost there.'

'Sadie you wander round in musty old clothes, quoting lines from dead fashion designers.'

'But they're vintage designer classics, Givenchy, Chanel, Schiaparelli, Balenciaga, and Dior. My grandmother gave them to me when she went into the nursing home.' I said feeling defeated. 'What else should I wear at the leading fashion school in the UK?'

'So your clothes are like a disguise, a uniform, an attempt to conform to the structure.'

'I guess, I do like them and they're beautifully made and the alternative is well, cheap schmutters from a fast fashion shop.'

'They kinda smell.'

'Smell,' I said nervously checking my armpit, 'what of?'

'Yes what is that smell, naphthalene?'

'What?'

'It's an insecticide; the proteins give off the vapour when they start to break down.'

'But what's the smell?' I gasped.

'Mothballs. You look okay today though.' She nodded reassuringly.

'Thanks,' I replied looking at my jeans and thinking I haven't tried at all today.

'I'm off to NFFW head office in Spain tomorrow. Then back to Afghanistan.'

'Why and what's all this jet setting about?'

'I've helped set up a co-operative clothing company in Afghanistan. We make embroidered koochie dresses and bags and are thinking of extending our range to quilted padded jackets.'

Joya stood up and pulled her coat off unleashing a rainbow of purple silk, with an intricate embroidered geometric pattern in blues, greens and various fiery reds and burnt sienna. The embroidery had been interwoven with gold and silver braids and tiny mirrors and beads had been added.

Joya continued, 'I have a meeting with NFFW tomorrow to see if they will sell our range. It's called Pashtun Braid.'

'Are NFFW going for it?' I asked tracing the design with my finger 'Isn't it against all the principles of fast fashion, pile it high and sell it cheap?'

'Well hopefully they will. I have already sent them all the literature and they haven't said no yet.'

'Sounds promising,' I added in a bemused way. Was fast fashion gaining a conscience?

I offered Joya a gluten free rice cake.

Joya sort of growled as she looked at the 'Haute' magazine opened on the richest people list and said, 'When I was in New York last week I was talking to Jenni one of the head buyers at Lackeys. I told her I worked at the Wonder Fashion School. She said her mother had worked at the Wonder factory in the late fifties.'

'Where Bill made his first Wonder Girdle?' I replied.

'Yes. She called later and invited me to a Fighting Cholitas wrestling event. It was a great night out. Her mother and some of her friends were there and we all got steaming drunk.'

'Sounds cool,' I said whilst enthusiastically rummaging through an old filing cabinet.

'The general consensus was that the Wonder factory was an okayish place to work but there were some oddities.'

'Like what,' I replied, picking up a traditional Chinese women's qipao and offering it to Joya.

'Most of them were experienced seamstresses and had worked in other sweatshops before, but at the Wonder factory they weren't making the finished garment, just pieces of it, more along the lines of a Ford production line I guess, and then rather mysteriously the pattern pieces were taken off and finished elsewhere so they never got to see the finished girdle.'

'Really, so they never saw a Wonder either,' I uttered in astonishment.

'No, they didn't, but when they did compare notes, they were all surprised by the size and cut of the sections they had to make. They didn't conform to the Berlei five standard sizes. The Hip spring was out. The waist to hip was far straighter than standard sizing. And most strangely, they had to add padding around the hips and bust. The girdles didn't actually suck you in, instead they rounded you off.'

'Maybe that's why they didn't sell many then,' I replied.

'Didn't they?' answered Joya surprised. 'The women all said they were very busy making their individual parts.'

'And what about the unconventional sized girdles. What does that mean?'

'Not sure,' Joya said, yawning.

'Joya have you seen the Dora Duffy mannequin dressed in a Wonder girdle outside Bill's new office?' I asked.

'You mean the very poor copy of a Wonder Girdle.'

I shrugged.

'I saw it when I went to HR this morning. It looks okay on a tiny plastic mannequin but if you look properly you'll see that there's no boning. It's just made out of material. And although I have never seen an actual Wonder Girdle I really can't see how that one would have changed the shape of anything.'

'So, even Bill doesn't have a copy of the Wonder girdle,' I gasped.

'I guess he doesn't,' Joya replied, putting the qipao in her bag. 'Thanks for this.'

'Thanks for not grassing me up,' I said humbly.

'No problem. I think I'll give that bitch Maggie Twill a right gob full before I leave.'

'Good. Oh and can you pretend to lock the plant room door and say something like there's no one in here.'

'Sadie, now you're thinking like management.'

'Thanks again,' I replied, feeling kowtowed.

'See you on the circuit amigo,' she smiled.

As Joya walked away, Tanya walked into the staffroom. She had changed into a Jacky Kennedy Chanel twinset and a Halston. Tanya had also added a gold bindi on her forehead and I think she may have had a lucky escape from Joya.

Tanya said, 'Err everyone; I'm sorry things are very disruptive at the moment but I ask you to act in a professional manner at all times.'

'Someone needs to cover Joya and Jonathon and Sadie lessons,' voiced practical Mags Twill. 'For that matter where is Sadie?'

'Yes and I'm sure you can manage it,' replied Tanya, 'just act in a professional manner.'

'At all times,' echoed Mags Twill looking a bit thunderous.

'That's right; oh yes it's Bill's funeral on Thursday. He will be buried in Highgate cemetery.'

'OOO, the ultimate burial address,' Maggie Cotton said rakishly. 'I wondered if he's secured a spot next to Karl Marx; they could argue capitalism versus socialism for eternity'.

'Yes thank you Maggie's,' continued Tanya, 'attendance is mandatory and so are hats. The other exciting news is that Sharleen from head office is coming to take over Bill's role.'

'What popping in every month and shouting?' smirked Mags Twill.

'I think she will be more hands on than that,' Tanya sobbed – and really looked like a suckling pig.

Chapter 9
Bubble Up

It was the day of the funeral and although I wasn't actually invited, I decided to go pay my respects, well really I was going to check that all the staff were at the funeral. I changed into one of my grandmother's oldest outfits, a 1920 Paul Poiret calf-length tunic dress in black velvet interwoven with a dove grey silk flower lame and accessorised with a black felt cloche hat with a crystal veil and a fox fur stole, which I suspect wasn't fake.

As I was paranoid about being recognised, I went all out on the heavy makeup and rubbed large amounts of the day of the dead white pan over my face and used a blood-red Cruella Deville lipstick on my cheeks. I took a good long look at myself before I left. I was definitely unrecognisable and looked rather like I had already died.

This I considered wholly appropriate for a funeral.

The sun was shining on the synagogue and as I watched the light fairies dance off the stained glass Star of David windows, I thought about one of my last memories of Bill the billionaire. The lighting system had suddenly failed and Bill's guest Martin Mansion, the CEO of Peter and Alison who was famous for his enforced hugging policy, had fallen over a box of £2 T-shirts. Bill had bellowed, 'You fat, ugly stupid emu,' at Tanya who technically was wearing a Saint Lawrence off the shoulder ostrich feather cocktail dress but as Bill was so angry, his face had gone purple, I felt it wouldn't be a good idea to correct his ratite mistake.

I was smirking about the incident and wondering how many other people in the congregation were thinking about similar happy memories of Bill when a voice said, 'Guess you weren't invited either.'

I turned and was greeted by a dapper older gentleman sitting in a wheelchair with a paisley cravat that matched his bright blue rheumy eyes.

'Not really,' I replied cagily.

'Schools, shops, factories, he certainly built an empire,' the old gentlemen said with a wry smile.'

'Yes, he did,' I replied not wishing to give anything away before I had figured out who he was. Then guessing the old gentleman was a man who would know the store, I said, 'I've been invited for tea at Dapplewhites, the department store, tomorrow.'

'Have you,' he replied, suddenly sounding very interested.

The old squire was sizing me up in a "guess the weight and size" way, and then said, 'That's where I met him, he was Solley Weitzman then.'

'Who's Solley Weitzman?' I asked.

'Him, the one in there, your Mr Bill Wonder, I knew him when he worked at Dapplewhites. Right clever bugger, spoke German and that made up secret Jewish language.'

'Yiddish,' I offered.

'Yes, that's right. He worked in the merchandising department. Then he got sacked over that funny business, you know, bit of a bufty. That's what Treadwell said. My name's Oswald Finlay by the way, pleased to make your acquaintance.'

'I'm Sadie Silver.'

Oswald sucked in his teeth, 'Related to Bobena Silver.'

'Yes, she's my grandmother.'

'Well, well, delighted to meet you my dear. Dapplewhites still has a photographic display of the Silver Franchise on the second floor just to the right of the lift. Filled with corsets, stockings, cami-knickers and the like,' he replied slightly lasciviously.

'Sorry, are you saying Bill Wonder was really called Solley Weitzman and worked at Dapplewhites?'

'Yes, I may be a pot and pan but I remember. I worked with Solley Weitzman for two years, 55-57. That bloke whose funeral we are both not really invited to is him alright.'

'And then he became Bill Wonder and made his money by designing the best corset in the world,' I mused.

'Yes, and I'll tell you another thing for free. Solley or Bill was best mates with your grandmother. Made Wilson mad, that did,' he said with a chuckle.

'Maude Wilson,' I interrupted.

'Yes, that's right. She could never find him whenever Bobena Silver visited. Solley was always scratching around her.'

My mind raced. Was the connection some sort of secret love child one? I choked out, 'Were they having an affair?'

Oswald chuckled, 'Don't think so, she was a fine-looking woman. No, it was lingerie, specifically corsets, that brought those two together.'

'Are you sure?' I frowned.

He chuckled whilst sucking his teeth, 'Oh yes, and then he became Bill Wonder and made his money by designing that Wonder girdle. Strange how he did that, given he was a number cruncher. Don't dismiss that though missy. It was a good job he landed, not many jobs like that for Jews in those days. He was smart. Not surprised he ended up a billionaire.'

'But he had no training in corsetière?' I questioned.

'Not that he told me. They threw him out you know. That Treadwell, Major Treadwell, new head of security dragged him through the shop. Treadwell… not thought about him for years, he was a right bastard, pardon my French. Fought in Malaysia … Chindit troop. Don't think he was right in the head afterwards. When he retired, he bought a cottage in the Cotswolds and called it after a bomb. He kicked Solley out on 24th October, 1957, at 11.30am.'

'That's precise.'

'That's me, good memory for the old days but to be fair, it was the day Cristobal Balenciaga launched his "sack" line. He was a right clever bugger too, foreshadowed the simple geometry of 1960s' fashion. Always remember that day.'

'And why did they kick him out?'

'Don't know, no one knew, some talk of him being a masher but no one ever really found out what had happened.'

'So you're saying that Bill Wonder was really called Solley Weitzman and he was sacked by Dapplewhites in 1957 for an unknown misdemeanour,' I replied trying to get this new information straight.

'Yes, it never really made sense to me either,' he nodded. 'But you did hear of stories like that one after the war. You know stories of people suddenly coming into vast fortunes for no reason, suddenly out of nowhere owning publishing empires or controlling vast pharmaceutical empires, usually in America. Dapplewhites imported all its whites from there and TVs, radios. Very strange really how that happened particularly as America was in recession just before the war.'

'What did you do after the war?'

'Went back to Dapplewhites, did well, I was head of men's outfitting,' he replied wistfully.

I was contemplating this new information and was about to question the old squire further when a young man with a tattooed face appeared and took hold of the wheelchair.

'Sorry about that, just needed to take a leak and didn't want to do it on the grave, who's your new friend? Been chatting up the ladies in my absence? I'm guessing he has been filling your head with his vintage retail stories again.'

'Yes, he has, but are they stories?' I questioned, looking at the old gentleman who now appeared to be napping.

'He's full of them, never know if they are true or not,' said the young man smiling. 'Bout time to go old fella, can't keep you out for too long. He insisted on coming, said the rich guy was an old acquaintance.'

Bill's service ended and the funeral possession made its way to the burial site. The procession was headed by a New Orleans' funeral dirge band, followed by an haute cortege of fashion models wearing torn designer black dresses and high sculptural headpieces and Bill's army of accountants who hadn't changed out of their grey polyester. Then finally the Wonder Empire staff and students trailed behind in a wispy black chiffon haze, abruptly disrupted by Harvey Dickens who in stark contrast had appeared in a shocking white suit and fedora hat. I could hear his sharp high voice saying, 'I read online that you do not have to wear black at a Jewish funeral.'

A stylistic reference towards the Baroque had taken hold, and variations of Marie Antoinette's iconic edifice of hair, a la Belle pouf, the perfect miniature copy of the frigate ship that had defeated the British in 1779, seemed to be the millinery of choice. Maria Antoinette YouTube hair style tutorials must have been accessed as several students had copied the pouf by folding their hair extensions into donuts and had added modern day vignettes. Someone had added a perfect miniature cash till; another had a clothes rack and several had created tiny balconies with miniature men in grey suits falling from them. One of the visual display students had copied the hair and the frigate and added a large wound around her neck.

I heard someone ask her, 'Is your outfit an anti-capitalist comment based on pseudo political hairstyles? Many historians have agreed that it was "Marie Antoinette hair vignettes", not the "let them eat cake" comment that did the House of Bourbon in the end.'

The girl looked bemused and replied, 'I copied it from the YouTube tutorial by Josephine French, called the "Halloween Marie Antoinette costume".'

As the cortège went on to Shiva, I decided to walk back to the office through Hackney Downs and take a look at the site where my grandmother's workshop had stood. A group of homeless people had gathered around with a shopping trolley filled with hipster cast-offs. I noticed a moustache comb and several NFFW flannel shirts and a box that said leg thinners. As I looked at them, I reflected on how homeless chic has bedded down in our fashion vernacular. The homeless had noticed me staring and one said jokingly, 'She thinks you look like Wei, that homeless man who became a model in China.'

'Yes, well I am rather gorgeous, I've got the razor-sharp cheekbones and his dark brooding good looks, what's it called? "Vagabond Sex Appeal",' said the first man.

'And you really understand layering?'

'And didn't he come to you for advice on his new woody, muddy, musky fragrance range?

'And of course, we can all pull off the shopping trolley accessory with effortless style,' replied the Wei one.

I added, 'Yes, fashion does seem to be commodifying poverty.'

They all stopped laughing and eyed me suspiciously, 'You an actress for one of them historical dramas, love? Have you lost your camper van?' laughed Mr Layer.

'Ahhh, you look just like someone from that family who owned the Silver workshop on Hackney Downs,' added the Wei look-alike staring at me intently.

'Yes, that's right; my grandmother Bobena Silver owned it.'

'What are you doing around here now?' asked Mr Layer, 'Not planning on resurrecting the Silver factory then?'

I shook my head.

'Shame, what with all the gentrification and London housing prices, there are plenty who could do with a job,' Wei added as I walked by.

I took the stairs to the third floor, the floor where Bill's accountants usually sat tapping out spreadsheets and where Bill's makeshift office was situated. As I opened the doors, several pale, silent and oddly still women eyeballed me with waxy gazes. I froze. Had I walked in on a post funeral surprise party attended by submissive mole women? I breathed again when it became apparent that they were not women but shop mannequins that had been arranged in a let's get up and greet you way. I appraised my unmoved hosts and it dawned on me that considerable thought had been put into the arrangement and dress of the ladies. Bill must have really liked playing fashion curator.

Not only had Bill arranged them chronologically, but had also appreciated that woman's hairstyles reflected the silhouette of their underwear in earlier centuries, which seemed to indicate a greater desire for erotic detail.

As I got closer to my goal, well Bill's school office, I saw mannequin Dora Duffy wearing the famous Wonder girdle. Dora stood on a plinth outside Bill's office and although Dora Duffy was a feisty up-for-it actress, her mannequin reincarnation managed to pull off a dignified-door-woman. I almost expected her to say, 'Good evening, madam. Would you like a drink?'

I studied the girdle, it was very pretty in a come-on-boys sort of way; a shocking pink black trimmed powerhouse of naughty but nice. But there was something about it that didn't quite say quality to me, something a little too mass produced, thrown together piecemeal, never mind the quality feel, the width to make me doubt that it could ever have become the most sought after girdle in the world.

'Joya was right,' I muttered. 'This mannequin Dora Duffy clearly has no fat on her moulded plastic body. But if she had, the material used to make this girdle has absolutely no sucking in properties at all. There's no vertical tension, no spring steel flats. Not even plastic synthetic whale bones.'

As I stepped back to visually re-appraise the slightly wanting Dora, something caught my eye at the back of Bill's office. I rattled the door but it was locked and then I rummaged through Josue's keys, none fitted. I stood on the Dora Duffy plinth and held onto the door frame and peered through the glass panel to get a better look.

On the wall above Bill's desk was a large silver framed painting. I pushed my face onto the glass panel and scrutinised the painting. Initially I thought it was an abstract minimalist work but if I half-closed my eyes and really stared at it, it began to take on the hazy shape of a corset. Its cut looked similar to the one on Dora Dufy but it somehow denoted a higher level of artisan quality than the shocking pink one. It seemed to say, 'Look at me, I am the original, the prototype, the master. Admire my proportions and corsetiere skill.'

As I peered in closer, Dora's plinth wobbled precariously and I grabbed the window sill to rebalance. When I refocused, the corset shape had gone and I was once again looking at a blank undistinguishable modern piece.

As I sniffed dismissively at the gaudy imposter whose plinth I was balancing on, Dora gazed back at me with her wide submissive eyes as if to say, 'Don't blame me, I didn't ask to be dressed in this tat.'

'So Dora,' I said whilst carefully clambering down, 'how am I going to get in Bill's office.' Dora didn't have an answer. As I walked back towards the tradesman's lift unsure of my next move, the under garmented mannequins looked a little sad, as if their only chance of salvation was now leaving, and a slightly grubby perhaps heroin chic mannequin, who smelt like wee wearing a wheat and straw braided Rumpelstiltskin corset seemed to say, 'Just leave it Sadie, you have already done enough to upset the status quo.'

Chapter 10
Cathedrals of Consumerism

I walked down Oxford Street to Dapplewhites with my invitation in hand. I had changed into a muted brown and green bird motif flower power floozy dress, which I had purloined from a mannequin in the side window display. I knew this was a bold move but it spoke Arts and Crafts to me, which I considered encapsulated Dapplewhites in its heyday nicely.

Oxford Street was still recovering from the Pepto riots and looked barren and post-apocalyptic. Tumbleweed balls of vibrant pink polyester blew across the empty grey urban shopscape, and the odd furtive pink faced fashionista would nervously scrapper out from boarded-up shop doorways and make a desperate grab for the tumbleweed before retreating to suck out the erythrosine. As I walked further down Oxford Street, the shops became predictably homogenised and Dapplewhites with its high turrets and flags stood out like an anachronistic fairy castle.

As I opened the heavy oak doors, I once again gazed in wonder. 'Oh, to the hallowed grounds of early consumer capitalism,' I sighed appreciatively.

I thought of the early euphoric days of consumer capitalism, textured so much by the department store. The women of the twenties and thirties thinking they had discovered a more exciting life. Their participation in the consumer experience challenging and subverting that complex of qualities traditionally known as feminine, dependence and passivity. The department store offered women their own space away from the home to carve out individual expression similar to men's workplace, pub or club. Places where women could look at things rather than being looked at, could meet friends, talk and stroll.

Department stores not only helped to redefine women's role by allowing them space to actively make decisions about consumption; many department stores, Dapplewhites included, had gone much further. They weren't just pitching sweets at children's eye level, forcing customers to walk around entire stores for just a few items, blocking their way with particular commodities, or folding clothing so customers are made to handle the items to see them. They were shrines, temples of consumerism where the complexities, tensions, and angst of everyday life could be simply brushed aside.

As I stood in reverence, a suave young man with a European accent approached me, nodded and enounced delightfully, 'Walk this way madam.'

I followed whilst looking up at the four circular balustrade floors of Pre-Raphaelite soap dishes, Bloomsbury group umbrellas; William Morris patterned scarves, caveats, riding crops with ivory fox heads and so many more white elephants, which lead harmoniously to a domed stained-glass roof which sparkled like the ascension to heaven. 'Dapplewhites really has turned shopping into a devotional rite confirming the ontological security of "I shop, therefore I am",' I muttered in reverence.

'Dapplewhites is one of the best early examples of the so-called cathedrals of modern capitalism,' the young man replied. 'She was built in 1908 and was very successful up to the fifties when the government introduced its agenda for tasteful consumption.'

'Yes, I imagine she had an uneasy relationship with the created by policy; colourless, pattern less, easy to mass produce and non-durable nature of Modernist design,' I agreed. 'Joya, my manager or maybe ex-manager always said, "The Festival of Britain was the beginning of the end for the working classes in this country, it's ideological social control through design," she would often growl.'

The young man looked a little confused but added, 'Having said that, the fashion cycle had come full circle and Dapplewhites' old English charm is now de rigueur, with a more global market and we have trouble keeping up with the endless Chinese demand for mackintoshes and green wellington boots.'

'Good,' I nodded.

He escorted me to the back of the shop and into an old lattice work lift to the basement, 'We are expanding into the basement,' he explained. 'The basement was used as a storage area for over eighty years and now we are clearing it, we keep discovering enchanting bygone relics. One could say like a shopping archaeological dig.'

'What's going to happen in the basement now?' I enquired.

'Oh turn it into flats. Basement flats, the building is so big we can make 20 pent or bent-house flats.'

'Are people going to buy flats in basements of shops?' I asked.

My Escort raised his eyebrow and pouted, 'Madame, they have been sold already. Mr Dapplewhites' financier suggested the idea and they all sold off plans the next day.'

How much?' I couldn't resist asking.

'Four to five,' he replied as he slid the lift door open.

I was greeted by a very excited Kimberley Clark. She was wearing an Alice through the Looking Glass outfit of blue dress and white pinafore with red and white striped stockings and brazen suspenders.

'Come, Sadie,' Kimberley said, 'Mr Dapplewhite is very keen to meet you.'

'Kimberley, why am I here?' I gasped starting to panic. Was she planning to use me in some sort of sexual double act?

Kimberley hooted with laughter, 'you're not here for that silly, besides you're too old and well a little too on edge, you would never pass any of my tests.'

I wasn't sure if I felt slighted or relieved.

'Mr Dapps and I were discussing the Bill business and I told him my favourite teacher Sadie Silver worked at the school. He was very surprised by your name and thinks he has found something that you will find interesting. Then we decided it would be fun to take tea in the basement before it's turned into flats,' she stopped to draw breath, 'So, that's why you're here, for tea and a chat.'

An elderly gentleman stood up to greet me, 'Well well, a genuine Silver. Ah I didn't think there were any left.' He stepped back and appraised me, 'You look just like your, let me think… grandmother Bobena, uncannily like her, uncannily.' He guffawed and so did Kimberly who nodded at me so I guffawed as well.

'Thought I had better say sorry to hear about that terrible business over at the school. Rum business, rum business.' He shook his head in disbelief, 'Well well well, Silver in the shop again. Father always said ask Bobena Silver if you're unsure about a range. Good at predicting a trend, fashion actuaries. Pure genius, pure genius.'

Kimberley poured tea and passed me the tiny floral teacup and nodded to indicate I should take a tiny pink fondant cake.

'So my dear,' Mr Daps continued whilst Kimberley rubbed the hot teapot up and down his thigh, 'whatever happened to Bobena Silver?'

'She moved to Devon and opened a ladies' dress shop,' I answered whilst trying to delicately balance my teacup and cake plate.

'Did she continue to make ladies lingerie?'

'No, she didn't.'

'I wonder why,' he said, turning his head at a curious angle.

Mr Dapplewhite smiled and patted my hand, 'She was the most formidable woman I have ever met. She used to scare the life out of me as a child. Used to pinch my cheeks and stare so intently, it felt like she could see into my soul.'

'Yes, that sounds like her.'

'One thing puzzles me,' he said

'Yes?' I gulped trying to appear unruffled.

'Erm, how shall I put this?'

Oh shit, I thought, anticipating his proposal.

He continued, 'Ermm, well my dear, why were you working for Bill Wonder?'

'Ohm, is that all?' I asked, relieved. Mr Dapplewhite looked a little puzzled and Kimberley dabbed a crumb of cake off his lips with a lacy handkerchief.

'Well I'm sure your grandmother wasn't pleased about that,' he said.

'Actually, you're right, she was really angry, called him a girdle stealing ferreter…'

'Well I think she may well be right,' Mr Dapplewhite chortled.

'I have a degree in fashion history, there weren't that many job opportunities,' I remonstrated.

'Well, now he's dead, I expect things will change at the Fashion school, change is as good as a rest they say.'

Kimberley tickled his chin and he quietly purred like a Cheshire cat.

'So Sadie, Kimberley tells me you were her favourite teacher. That's praise indeed as you clearly taught her many transposable skills,' he said whilst patting Kimberley's bottom.

Kimberley leant over dramatically and caught a cake crumb in her cleavage.

'I expect you are keen to know why you have been called to attend our little tea party.'

I nodded.

'Good, good. Well then, we have been clearing out old papers and packages in the basement; it's like an Aladdin's cave. I'm glad I waited so long to do it; it's so much more fun now that Kimberley is here to help.' Kimberley smiled and patted his balding head. 'We have found something that I believe could be of significance to a Silver. I wanted to pass them on but had no idea where they had ended up. Then my clever little caterpillar here said she knew the whereabouts of one.' He patted Kimberley's bottom affectionately and sipped his tea and nibbled pink icing from the top of a tiny cake.

'Voilà,' Kimberley said dramatically, producing two heavy dusty ledgers, 'Exhibit one.'

Kimberley sat on Mr Dapps lap and opened the first hand-written ledger, 'Three pairs of stockings, Cleopatra, Lovers Knot and Fire down below 20s 10D,' she said.

'That was your grandmother's ledger when she had her Dapplewhites franchise. I have no idea why she left it here. It would have made her tax returns rather difficult to fill. And this is one of my father's ledgers, he of course started Dapplewhites, I am just the son who inherited the fortune.'

'You're so much more than that, doopy woopy,' said Kimberley tickling his chin.

Mr Dapplewhite pointed to an entry dated 31st December 1956, 'Read that part please Kimberley.'

'Received: One sample corset from the Silver Lingerie Workshop.

Dapplewhites have given a down payment of 100 guineas on the condition that they have sole retail rights,' Kimberley said with authority.

I looked up at Mr Dapplewhite, 'I remember my father telling me how excited he was about this corset. He said it was the future, well the next 10 years which is a very long time in fashion and then he gave me a quarter of aniseed balls and told me not to blow up any limpet mines.' Mr Dapplewhite guffawed.

Kimberley put the ledger in an old cream Dapplewhites hat box and passed it to me, 'It's a present for you Sadie, put it to good use. It's all going to be thrown out so don't worry.'

Mr Dapplewhite finished his tea and gave me a retailer's up and down stare and I could tell he saw something wanting in me; chutzpah maybe. 'Goodness gracious me, my hour's nearly up,' he said clearly indicating our tea party had finished, 'Come my dear it's time for indoor croquet on the Queen's Roof Terrace.'

Just before they went, I thought of something, 'Mr Dapplewhite, did a Solley Weitzman ever work here or for that matter an Oswald Finlay.'

'Oswald Finlay, yes, fine chap, men's outfitting, the other I'm not sure about,' he answered in a distracted way as

Kimberley was now pretending to play hopscotch with her skirt mysteriously tucked into her bloomers.

Kimberley mouthed sorry and added a call me hand sign before they both gambolled away.

I stood in the empty basement holding the Dapplewhites hat box unsure what to do next. Then as if by magic, the suave young man appeared beside me and said, 'Mr Dapplewhite asked me to escort you out as he is sure you have lots of work to do.'

I followed the young man to the lift, lost in thought. As we exited, he asked breathlessly, 'Do you work with Jonathon Longbottom? Do you think he did it? Did you see Bill Wonder fall?'

'I really don't know,' I responded wearily.

'Jonathon worked here you know. He designed the UM bag window; he's sort of famous here. Although admitting you bought a UM bag is a bit like admitting you liked the Spice Girls now,' he said whilst pointing to a wall that had the slogan, "The perfect weave for material happiness" scrolled in mock fountain pen effect.

He shook his head in disbelief, 'What ridiculous self-obsessed marketing trivia,' he scowled.

'Maybe you need to save the world rather than working in a department store,' I smiled.

'Maybe,' he replied, waving me out.

I opened the heavy doors and stepped away from the castle of consumer dreams and hurried down Regent Street. The box awkwardly balanced in my outstretched hands.

Chapter 11
The Underground

As I walked back to Soho, the streets of London, which are ordinarily filled with buses and taxis, had been taken over by party people. A lorry was driving past carrying a large DJ mixer set and a girl sprayed gold. Walking along next to the lorry singing, 'We are family' was a band of merry superheroes. There was the hunked up metal android complete with a gun belt and extra-large ray gun. A muscular action figure clad in a black bodysuit with white stars and a blue shapeshifter holding hands with a precog dressed in an ethereal grey sheath. The lorry was closely followed by the third political party marching as Priscilla, queen of the desert with a purple and lavender mini bus. The leader of the party wore a white and pink feather headdress and white thong and a sequinned bra. Marching next to him was the Minister for Justice in a yellow corset with yellow and orange pompoms and a headdress made out of lemons. Several other politicians followed dressed in corsets and feather head dresses. They moved elegantly in their high heeled boots. Every few minutes they did a little gender reframing shimmy. The next float was carrying staff from a well-known bank that I think was playing to the idea that identity is entirely malleable and open to radical redefinition. This may have also reflected their banking practices. Rotund balding bank managers with Ziggy orange mullet hairpieces and white rice powder faces and black kohl eyes snaked and air-guitared. And a paunchy little man in a multi coloured knitted jumpsuit and a turquoise feather boa carried a banner that read, 'Imagination and sexual desire matter more than gender and sexual orientation? I was a little underwhelmed by the next float which seemed to have gone past gender reframing and ended up performing genderless heteronormativity as they all marched in unison in grey charcoal suits and short back and sides.

Then I remembered today was Pride.

I was carried on the good cheer to Belgravia Square which looked like a gigantic picnic, a street performance Yoko Ono was enacting the 1964 cut piece but the audience although holding scissors were not cutting away at her dress and were instead cutting flowers shapes out of Best Girl plastic bags which they were delicately wrapping round the very surprised Yoko.

And a group of Fred and Fred Astaire dressed in tuxedos with bow ties black and white saddle shoes and top hats and canes were ballroom dancing around the square.

I was going to sit down on an empty bench when a group of people whistled and shouted, 'Yeah, William Morris, come sit with us.'

They were all dressed in diaphanous romantic Ossie Clark and Celia Birtwell outfits. They offered me a cool beer and some crisps.

'I like your arts and crafts outfit. But why are you holding a hatbox?' Asked one dressed in a floral peach and black maxi.

Rather than go into a detailed explanation I flippantly replied 'I'm no longer sure what to wear now that fashion discourses are dead.'

'Yes, you're right it's very hard to decide what to wear now. We spent ages deciding on these outfits. But I'm still not sure whether they situate the self or send culturally coded messages to others,' one said.

' I really have no idea what to wear now that the Wonder Empire has stopped flooding me with subtle sumptuary manoeuvres and tactics,' replied someone dressed in a two-piece floral print flared tunic trimmed with an orange satin neck-tie.

'Yes it's a bit like someone has opened the gates of Jeremy Bentham Panopticon very suddenly and we have no idea what to do with free will,' added someone dressed in fluid ethereal yellow, green and black trouser suit

'Are we missing our cruel master now?' Laughed the floral peach.

'Yes, I guess as fashion is the perfect embodiment of the new modern aesthetic now that we have no power exercised over us it is becoming confusing,' I added.

'Actually I completely disagree. The hyper reality of the computer game is the aesthetic of our time and therefore fashion is now obsolete,' replied the person dressed in floral.

I acquiesced, mainly because I know nothing about computer games but did add, 'You all look very pretty though.' And we all agreed on that.

The group told me they ran a music collective and gave me a flyer for a music event at the House of Charity and pointed out that it was just at the other side of the square. When they left I walked over. I had seen a TV documentary about its elaborate Rococo plasterwork which is one of the best examples of English Rococo plasterwork left in the UK. I was fascinated by its staircase known as the Crinoline stairs and a room called the withdrawing room. I stood outside and smelt coffee and I followed the smell and went inside. The House of Charity was holding a charity event to raise funds to protect the plasterwork and the organisers were dressed as characters from Charles Dickens novels. The Entrance Hall was rather plain and I felt a bit cheated and then a Chelsea posh dissolute artsy man appeared wearing a Mr Sowerberry outfit and very enthusiastically said, 'I like your hat box handbag. It needs straps though. I bet you want a tour.'

I really didn't but it looked like I was getting one.

'The simple decoration of the hall was a deliberate device to attract the visitor's eye to the decorated staircase leading to the rooms on the first floor,' said my guide as he ushered me upstairs. 'The wrought-iron staircase balustrades are original. And this Angel on the landing is the oldest object in the house. It dates from the 1600s; it's made of wood and is Flemish.'

I nodded and smiled as we headed to the drawing room, 'The ceiling as you can see has four female busts. The central oval medallion shows four cherubs holding in their hands the symbols of the four classic elements; water, fire, air and earth. Over here we have two dragons made of papier-mâché, of the city of London. And over here we have the electro level beams, tilt sensors and precise levelling points which feed data on movement back to headquarters every 15 minutes to provide critical twist information during localised compensation grouting works.'

'What?' I said wondering if I had misheard.

'Data on movement,' repeated the dissolute artsy Mr Sowerberry.

'Yes, but why?'

'Look at all the building work going on around here. And that's not the only problem. They keep digging underneath this part of London and any movement affects the plasterwork.'

'Has there been movement?' I asked looking down the spiral staircase nervously.

'Well yes, you don't build gigantic tunnels big enough to fit trains in without causing movement; the House of Charity is being monitored because of the priceless plasterwork.'

'Oh, that's terrible,' I replied unsure of the etiquette.

'Here take this; it's the House of Charity newspaper. It explains it all in black and white.'

'Thanks.'

'Err, we usually ask for a donation for the tour and the newspaper.'

I reluctantly handed him a pound.

'Thanks, the café is down the hall,' he replied whilst heading out the front door.

I brought a ridiculously expensive coffee and salted caramel slice and read through the newspaper. The House of

Charity; charity volunteers were understandably concerned that their Grade 1 listed Georgian stucco plasterwork, which was irreplaceable and particularly sensitive to subsidence, was being destroyed by the Brobdingnagian underworld and had installed a bespoke stucco monitoring system which was particularly sensitive to any movement and would send alarm signals to tunnel control, who would immediately pump liquid concrete through uber fine pipes to settle everything down.

Engineering is very reassuring I thought, much more tangible than fashion. The article was followed by a colour coded map of underground sink spots with a vector graph, where you could trace the times and dates for the worst-affected buildings. The brightest coloured hotspot by far, occurred four days ago at 8.59 am. And according to the tunnels' timeline graphic of a beaver with giant teeth, the earth pressure balance drill was boring exactly underneath the Fashion school then. If the graph of beavers with safety helmets and headphones falling into the abyss was to be believed, the vibration from the one-ton boring drill could have caused considerable vibrations, noise and possibly movement to the building above and many beavers would have fallen from it.

Four days ago at 8.59 am was a date and time that had been chiselled out in my perplexed brain, because it was of course the exact time and day that Bill had fallen from his fashion fortress. Had the new world order attacked from below?

From the underground?

A place Bill had never managed to penetrate with his mid-range fashion stores?

If this were the case, could Bill have just fallen over the balcony?

Chapter 12
False Consciousness

I sat on the tube and read through my grandmother's heavy ledger. From what I could make out, the Silver Franchise at Dapplewhites was extraordinarily successful. Each day there were over thirty transactions for stockings, garters, long line bras, full corsets, firm control corsets, 2 way stretch girdles, sarong girdles, panty girdles, corselets and several entries for falsies. I roughly calculated that she must have been turning over about £60 a week. It really didn't make any sense that she would suddenly up and leave.

I got home and put the ledgers on the kitchen table and sat down and mulled. Did my accidental purloining of Bill's photographic collection of scrawny young men put in motion a chain of events that had started in 1957 and led to his death sixty years later? And if so, how was my grandmother involved? If everything was connected, it would seem to have started at Dapplewhites and all be tied up with the Wonder Girdle.

I groaned with confusion and then vaguely thought about telling the police but changed my mind at the thought of the police saying, something like, 'So madam, you think Bill's death is related to a 1950s corset franchise and a photograph album of semi naked young men. What concerns me more is why you didn't come forward earlier and why you ran away from the scene of the crime in the first place?'

No, going to the police now really wasn't going to work but I could do with some help. What I needed was a clever person who had moved beyond the black and white dichotomy of crime and punishment. I rattled through my list of wise, non-judgemental friends or acquaintances but couldn't think of anyone, well apart from my grandmother. Then as if by magic or algorithm, I noticed a rerun of the Judith Trousers' Pepto report on TV and I rang the university and asked to be put through. She answered as if she didn't quite believe that telephones work, 'Hello, hello is anyone there?'

'Yes, it's Sadie Silver.'

'Silver,' she shouted and then the phone went dead.

I waited a few minutes and then rang back. She answered immediately, 'Oh I'm glad you called back, the university has re-structured and told the administrative staff they have to work harder for less pay so they all just left. Between you and me, I am not sure what buttons to press on a telephone, never mind how to operate those white board thingies. It's chaos here. So Sadie, how are you? I haven't heard from you in what, about five years now. What are you doing now?'

'I'm teaching at Bill's fashion school or at least I was...' I began.

'Oooh yes, I'm surprised it took so long for someone to push him off the balcony,' she replied.

'I'm interested in Bill Wonder's girdle factory in New York, where he made the Wonder girdle,' I replied, trying not to get embroiled in a Bill's death conversation.

'Of course you are, aren't we all,' she answered mysteriously.

'Are we all?'

'Yes, you want to know if it was just a girdle factory, don't you.'

'Yes, I suppose I do,' I replied somewhat surprised.

'Can you come in and chat? I'm free tomorrow at 12.'

'Thanks, that's great,' I replied happily. I love it when a plan comes together.

As I had nothing much to do in the morning, I walked to the school. As I approached, I had to stop and do a double take. The students had created a new and even more unsettling shop window display. Window shopping used to be central to the processes of consumption. It allowed the consumer to create fantasies and get pleasure in the processes of desiring goods rather than actually buying them. I wasn't sure if the students had achieved quite the right balance here. I assumed the project brief must have been along the lines of psychosexual maladroit florals.

Most of the mannequins were naked apart from awkward leather straps wrapped around their breasts or buttocks, some I noticed (presumably the vegans among the group), had used PVC or rubber. There was a bondage bride lying Pre-Raphaelite prone, in a rusty old bathtub holding a mirror. She wore a bondage harness in black leather which exposed her stomach and breasts. Her full skirt escaping the bath's darkened water, overflowed in a brambly mesh of black taffeta and dead roses.

The second window was a communal garden dominatrix dungeon. A mannequin spread eagle on a bed of nails with her sexless genitals on display, looking very much like Barbie does pain. A second mannequin looming over in a flowery, peekaboo baby doll nightie and fuck-me boots. The standing mannequin was holding a silver jug and presumably pouring something that was meant to be corrosive hot wax or acid, onto the face of the nail-bedded one. The corrosive effect, which I assumed was executed before the shop window staging as is, was now a piece of blue plastic and the mannequin's plastic face had melted down one side to create a grotesque, late stage pox-afflicted effect. I was pondering how effective a marketing tool the window display was for mid-range fashion, when I almost bumped into Sharleen getting out of a black cab. I quickly hid myself behind my hermitage, the industrial bin.

Sharleen from head office was like a minute, evil gone wrong, fairy godmother. If you looked at her from afar, she looked tiny and elfin slim and possibly even cute. But when you were in spitting distance, she was compellingly scary. Her hands and feet were extraordinarily large for a tiny person and her jawline had that Desperate Dan slant. She was a person to be avoided at all costs, her very presence seemed to cause waves of unhappiness in those around her, despite her ability to hyper emote ill feeling, she wasn't clever or well read, or had American CEO charisma. Her effectiveness was based on her ability to be so objectionable that the best way to escape her was to do what she said immediately. Bill had loved her, unusually for a very successful businessman, there wasn't a smidgeon of misogynist about him, and you could call him anti misogynist, a true feminist. He loved nothing more than to be surrounded by loud, domineering obnoxious women.

As I peeked through the space between the two bins, I noted that Sharleen had dropped a photocopy of a PowerPoint presentation entitled "New Vision", no doubt Sharleen's new plan for the school. Slide one said, "to enhance the workplace experience, the school will become a limited company and all students will be partners in the business with full financial responsibility". The next slide read, "the fashion design students will now produce fully manufactured and shop ready clothes. Aadit Dhillon, one of the most successful clothing factory owners in India, will help set up and oversee production. Buying and merchandising students will be responsible for allocation; sourcing and ensuring ranges appear in the shop – right product, right time, right price. Visual display students will run all marketing". At the bottom of the slide rang the tagline, "Wonder bank is offering very reasonable loans but will require guarantors".

Sharleen turned to the taxi driver, 'Just put it on the tab and pick me up at the Rosewood hotel same time tomorrow,' she said whilst toppling past in her fuck-me boots.

I had prepared for my meeting with Judith Trouser by dressing as a mock intellectual "Daphne" from Scooby Doo and to that end was wearing woolly stockings, a three-quarter length tweed skirt, tank top and heavy rimmed glasses. I was confident that clever anarchic old Judith would get the joke. As I entered the hallowed grounds of my alma mater "the Fashion University or FU" as we students had affectionately called it, I thought back to when I had moved to London from Devon as an eighteen-year-old. It was sort of exciting but on the whole, it was really quite horrible. I never had enough money and was forced to live in terrible, cold, miserable student housing, eat crap food and learn to avoid the sort of people that I had previously thought only existed in box sets about run-down areas of America. Still I guess it was all worth it in the end. And 60k of student debt with interest of 6% is nothing given that I had after all landed my dream job at the Fashion School, even though I had now lost it and I'm not actually sure it was ever that dreamy.

'Sadie, nice to see you. So did you say you were still working at the terrible school?' asked Judith Trouser as she waved me into her office. Judith's tiny, ancient, owl-like face appeared over piles of essays, books and loose papers.

'Actually I don't really know,' I answered in an abstract way.

Judith laughed gustily, 'How brilliantly self-determining of you,' she said with oodles of good cheer.

I removed a pile of paper from a chair and sat down. Judith gave me a short-sighted stare. 'So you have come about the mythical Wonder girdle. The myth that naturalises the ideology. Don't go chasing it. You will never find one, rather like the crock of gold.'

'Why do you say that? Isn't it how Bill Wonder made his billions?'

'I don't think Bill Wonder made his money from the Wonder girdle as a commodity, well a commodity with extrinsic goods value, that is.'

'What do you mean?' I replied although I wasn't surprised by Judith's thinking.

Judith confirmed my own views on the girdle, 'I have never met a woman who claims she had a Wonder girdle. Many have admitted to a Spirella or a Spencer and even a Silhouette but never a Wonder, and I have interviewed thousands of them. It's the emperor's new clothes of girdles. I tried to find one once. I searched everywhere. Finally I was contacted by a military historian in Germany. He claimed to have found one in Dusseldorf. He wouldn't part with it though. So I could never authenticate it. Why are you so interested in it? Ooo do you think it has something to do with Bill's death? Strangled by his own creation… ooo how very

Frankenstein,' she cooed then leaned in and said whilst tapping her nose, 'Of course my suspicion is that it never actually did anything for the silhouette, never actually did a thing.'

'But it was so successful, one in every three women in the western world had one,' I gasped.

'Did they Sadie. Let's think about America in the late fifties, early sixties,' she said opening her arms widely, as if by doing so she would create a pop-up country.

I grinned as I remembered why I enjoyed her contextual studies lectures so much.

'America leads the way in the social science experiment known as marketing.' She nodded knowingly and then lent in confidently, 'America's war trophies not only included eminent European scientists and pharmacists but most of the intellectuals from the Institute of social research at the Goethe University in Frankfurt. Their work on behavioural science, particularly the sociology of social control through mass culture, was paramount in changing consumer ideology. It must have been like taking candy from a baby back then.' Judith chuckled, 'So, so much scope for re-establishing the social order. Of course it can take two forms; compliance or resistance but on the whole, it was total obedient compliance.' She said nodding rigorously. 'America benefited from the Second World on so many levels, so many levels. I wouldn't be surprised if they started it. Of course the British complained, and made documentaries about whales and obscure ethnic groups instead. But where did that get them?'

'You mean films like Dora Duffy in *Naked Corset* with her contradictory ideas about feminine innocence and sexiness?'

'Precisely, it was all marketing usually driven by political agendas.'

'So all the "fit your foundations before your frocks", promulgating, really was just consumer driven propaganda but for what, if not Wonder girdles?'

'Think advertising, marketing, false consciousness, subtle coercive theories. One in three women allegedly bought a

Wonder girdle but recent social research would suggest that this wasn't the case.'

I managed a coherent, 'Really, how interesting.'

'Exactly,' she replied looking very intellectually satisfied. 'What have you got there?'

I produced the accounts ledger from the Silver franchise at Dapplewhites and the photograph album. Judith studied them hungrily, 'Well, well, well and yet another piece of the puzzle but does it help or does it hinder? Did your grandmother know Bill Wonder?'

'Yes, I think she did.'

'Your grandmother's franchise was very profitable,' she nodded, 'surprisingly profitable really.'

'What do you mean?' I queried.

'Well it was the point I was getting at a minute ago, your grandmother wasn't mass producing her corsets. She was a corset maker, a corsetiere, a highly skilled craftsperson. She wasn't working to a standardised sizing formula. She was hand making each one individually based on the carefully measured body shape of every customer. Everyone would have been a bit different to fit each client's unique body shape. And she seemed to be, well, knocking them out.'

'Yes, I suppose she did,' I replied looking through the ledger receipts, 'and wait, are you also telling me that mass produced standardised girdles didn't actually work? Isn't that how Bill made his first million?'

'Well they worked occasionally when the odd completely standardised woman tried one on. I have never come across an algorithm to give a percentage for this but I expect it's quite low. How many women do you know that are exactly the same height and width as you?'

'None, now that you mention it,' I said. 'But every woman in the late fifties had a Wonder girdle. You were considered improperly dressed without one.'

'In the 1950s the Berlei Company conducted an anthropometric survey of women's body sizes and concluded that all women fitted into one of five basic figure types, and from this a system of sizing was developed. It was very standardised and made sound economic sense and soon after, all mass-produced clothing was made to these standards. And interestingly, the term corset was lost to the new more fashionable word girdle, but really it never actually worked,' Judith informed me knowledgeably.

'And then suddenly everyone was burning their bras and wearing miniskirts,' I added.

'Smoke and mirrors all smoke and mirrors,' she nodded sagely, 'but all conjecture because no one has actually seen a Wonder.'

Judith's phone rang at that moment, 'Yes, I'm coming,' she shouted. 'Sorry, I have to dash. I was due in a meeting fifteen minutes ago. Sadie, it was good to see you. Keep in touch.'

I nodded doubting her ability to contact me unless she intended to use a carrier pigeon and then said, 'But Judith, you didn't look at the photograph album.'

As I walked down Mallet Street, it dawned on me that I had no idea what was happening in the world, what was trending, what handbags were in our out, whether I should be wearing pastels, florals, monochrome or yellow. Had I inadvertently moved down a tier in Maslow's hierarchy of needs? Or was I slowly weaning myself off the most addictive of drugs, consumer fetishism?

When I got home, I had a rethink. Although I had discovered many things, I wasn't sure if I was closer to the truth or further away. If Judith was right and Bill's Wonder girdle was just a figment of false advertising, how had he managed to maintain the illusion for so long? Surely by now, fifty years later, there would have been an exposé, a Daily Mail shock horror scandal. I mean I know women born before the millennium aren't given to complaining but surely at least one would have kicked off about it. Or maybe one did kick off… in a push the greedy billionaire off the balcony kind of way. I felt a little pang of sympathy for poor Jonathan wallowing in jail, but it passed very quickly.

I changed into the ever so comfortable vintage Chanel; it really needed a wash and smelled mildly of anxiety BO, which could be mine or the previous owner's. If clothes are the outward manifestation of inward pain, the vintage Chanel was telling me things hadn't been quite right for a while now. I thought about whether Chanel and my Bubbe would have got on? They would have clashed on silhouettes.

'Hourglass my derriere,' Chanel would say.

'Boyish figure my tokhis,' Bubbe would reply.

They may have got on to how Chanel survived the war and the moral implications of sleeping with the enemy to ensure your clothing legacy. They would no doubt disagree on that too. Chanel didn't hold back, would do anything no matter how despicable to ensure her fashion destiny. My Bubbe chose to surrender. What could have spooked her so much? It was unlikely to be a man; she never took much notice of them. My grandfather was bookish and kind and never dared do anything to annoy her. Maybe an institution or a government, she always had an innate mistrust of large organisations. 'Administrations have no soul or humanity, Sadie. They simply fill in small pieces of big pictures and never see the consequences of their actions.'

Chapter 13
Overexposure

I slept the sleep of the accused and my Kafkaesque dream started with a voice saying, 'One day you will get arrested.'

'Why?' I ask desperately.

A shopkeeper points to my feet. I look down. I'm standing on a mountain peak made up of designer shoes and handbags. I protest my innocence but now a policeman has appeared and calmly says, 'How can you be innocent? You are guilty of fashion crimes. You have bought into an institutionally constructed, culturally diffused symbolic belief system. Unless you can prove you were not competent when you purchased your fashion mountain, you will go to prison for a long time.'

I opened my eyes and panicked. I was going to get arrested, why, for what? Was it for dressing in the clothes of the constructed discourses of a western political, social and economic system? Surely that's called being a good citizen, fitting into the expected social norms of the society you live in. Or do we get arrested for conformity now? Maybe it was the small details that I would be punished for, the embellishments, not understanding the difference between mass produced girdles and handmade corsets, buying into advertising propaganda unquestionably. Being in the wrong place at the wrong time when a billionaire fell from a balcony. And something else, something that for some reason I can't quite grasp. But it was clearly something to do with my grandmother's corset workshop and Bill Wonders Empire.

I needed to think so went in search of cultural diversions. I have always found staring at relics from the past incredibly meditative. Interestingly, modern art doesn't do this for me at all. It's all a bit more narcissist and seems to shout, 'Look at me, I'm the artist and I'm way too self-obsessed to comment about anything other than myself.'

The British museum was busy and as the sun was shining, I sat on the steps, closed my eyes and basked lizard like. I was trying to figure out what had scared Bobena so much that she ran away from the cash cow Silver franchise at Dapplewhites, when I heard voices that I recognised. Standing at a hearable distance were the voices – ergo bodies – of three Fashion school students Efi, Sammy and Jaz, and I'm pretty sure they were talking to Polly Rootbeer, the YouTube high priestess of subcultural cool who had single handiily invented the Neanderthal eyebrow and face contour look.

Polly sounded whiny and desperate, and the ex-teacher in me sensed there was more to this little gathering than met the eye.

I snuffled down a few steps and inquisitively eavesdropped. The three students looked frustrated and annoyed and Polly Rootbeer was a bit weepy. I wondered if they were arguing over creativity; possibly one of Polly's brilliant self-reflective windows on the world, multi-platform media art pieces. But if so, how would it involve the students?

Efi was saying, 'But everyone at the show had a phone in their hand and their snapchat accounts primed, why are we being blamed? There was total transparency; it was a socially shared experience.'

Polly pulled a duck face and said, 'But now everyone knows about the two aspects of my piece. '

'You mean the *Trompe l'oeil,* tribute to Elsa Schiaparelli and how the photograph, the 2-dimensional image, has become more important than the actual garment, the actual 3D product.' Sammy smirked.

'Are you mocking my Bashion concept?' Polly said angrily.

'Our Bashion concept,' Efi added.

'Well technically, I think it's Miyake industries,' corrected Sammy.

Polly let out a sob, and then continued on her whiny diatribe, 'I wanted Bashion to demonstrate how things have changed in the last five years. How the digital screen now forms the cornerstone of modern consumer culture, and all clothes are viewed as flat images.' She breathed in and revved up the whine. 'How online oversharing has made the image and not the object the ultimate commodity. Now with hundreds, probably thousands of clips of 2D fashion all over social media sharing platforms, how can my concept work?'

'Our concept, and don't you think this makes it more poignant, remember we are commenting on the image and the sharing experience; how the image has simultaneously become the vehicle, context, content and commodity, the most important thing is not the dress or in this case the boiler suit. You could see this as a blow or you could view it as good timing,' Efi replied

'There's no such thing as bad publicity,' added Sammy patronisingly.

Polly snorted and added doubtfully, 'So my 3D or even 4D fashion art performance boiler suit, in which I wanted to make people aware of image overexposure, is enhanced by social media overexposure?'

'Yes,' the students said in unison.

Polly was unconvinced, 'But the back of the *Trompe L'oeil* dresses actually look like cut out paper dolls and everyone loves them and posts their favourite.' She started to sob.

Efi tried once again to reason with her, Jaz and Sammy looked thoroughly bored. 'Yes, I know, we came up with the concept remember.'

Polly didn't look like she remembered this at all.

Efi bravely reasoned on, 'Because a fashion show is now calibrated to be a socially shared experience, we can't control who films it, we can't block all mobiles, destroy all the photos, it may be a problem if it undermines our project, but I don't think it does.'

Sammy interjected perhaps unkindly, 'I have to say, when the models walked down the runway wearing their 2-

dimensional dresses taking photographs of the audience, that was a real "in your face" moment.'

Sammy's comment enraged Polly even more. 'Well if you think it's a joke, how about I don't pay you,' she said in an even whinier way.

Rather than grovelling and saying sorry, we will fix it, we need your money, the students sniggered and walked off.

So, Polly Rootbeer has been paying students for creative ideas. Is nothing sacred I thought?

'As I stood up I bumped into Mr Dapplewhite. Mr Dapplewhite was holding an ice cream which was now dripping down my Chanel.

'Well I never. If it isn't Bobena Silver,' he said looking aghast, 'I thought you died.'

'It's Sadie, Sadie Silver her granddaughter,' I replied. 'Remember, we met in the Dapplewhites basement. And actually Bobena isn't dead, not just yet anyway.'

'Yes, of course,' he replied. 'Oh good, that must mean I haven't died either. Mind you, not a bad way to go on a sunny afternoon on the steps of the British museum, ice cream and pretty girl, mmm woman in tow.' Mr Dapplewhite took out a neat chequered handkerchief and handed it to me to wipe the sloppy ice cream remains. 'Would you like a coffee? I need to sit down after that.'

We went in and Mr Dapplewhite pushed to the front of the queue and as he was a dapper older gentleman, no one minded and some Chinese tourists took photographs of him.

'I'm very interested to hear how you've been getting on,' he said, passing me a coffee and a bun.

'Thanks. I'm not really sure I'm making any progress.' I replied a bit despondently.

He looked at me and seemed disappointed. 'Business was good, there really was no reason why your grandmother took off like that and you say to Devon, of all places.'

' When Kimberley told me who you were, I was happy to help. Your grandmother was such a well, shall we say character, independent, clever, very good at commerce and very direct,' he chortled reminiscently. 'Oh I almost forgot,

Kimberley and I did some digging on your Solley Weitzman. Solley Weitzman did work at Dapplewhites in merchandising but well, I don't like to say this but he was a wrong un. Rather rum business, rather rum. He was clever. But I think, shall we say he had some rather unusual sexual proclivities. Kimberley said she would call you and tell you all about it.' He looked at his watch and said, 'Goodness, look at the time. It was delightful to meet you again Sadie, I hope the ice cream will wash out.'

I looked down at my jacket; the ice cream had merged in quite well. Mr Dapplewhite stood and said, 'And if there's anything else I can do, please contact my secretary. Kimberley, your student Kimberley, now she's quite a girl,' he chuckled as he hurried off.

I finished my coffee and appreciated Norman Foster's great domed canopy. I noticed a poster for a synthetic fabric dye exhibition on the third floor and decided a study of man-made colour was exactly what I needed. The first exhibit focussed on natural dyes. I read the information sheet written in a mock Victorian ink pen. "From ancient times up to the middle of the nineteenth century, all dyes were made from a variety of natural sources, ranging from plants such as roots, berries, flower heads, or leaves, minerals and trees, especially barks, lichens and insects. For example, most red dyes were derived from plants such as madder, beetroot, cranberry, safflower, and orchid; and a few more valuable ones from insects such as cochineal from Central America. Yellows were extracted from Persian berries, weld, dyers broom and saffron. Despite its seemingly natural abundance, green could only be obtained by double-dyeing with fustic yellow and indigo blue." The display cabinet contained various examples of flowering leguminous plants, madder roses and bird pooh.

The next cabinet debated the environmental impact of natural dyes which were by all accounts a nasty business with significant environmental impact. I read a report from the notebook on an Ezra Weld in Florida 1715. 'The stench of the work vats, where the indigo plants were putrefied, is so offensive and deleterious, that we have had to move the workers' tents one quarter of a mile away. The odour from the rotting weeds drew flies and other insects by the thousands, greatly increasing the chances of the spread of diseases.' Ezra had added hand drawn illustrations of exhausted workers pushing large paddle-like spoons in gigantic cauldrons and buckets of noxious waste being dumped into a river.

The next section of the exhibit called "Mauveine" lent itself to a lovely shade of purple and focused on the beginning of the synthetic dye industry. Financially, Fabric dyes were a vast global business which originally started on the actual Silk Road not the virtual one. Natural Indigo came from the Middle East and Africa and can be dated back to 3000 BC before traders introduced it to the Mediterranean region during the 11th Century. The first artificial mauveine dye was developed by William Henry Perkin in 1856 by extracting aniline from black coal. Perkins was an English chemist and whilst trying to synthesise quinine, accidentally discovered mauveine. Perkins failed in his treatment for malaria but succeeded in the colour purple, the colour of kings since ancient times. He called his dye Tyrian purple, and when Queen Victoria and Empress Eugenie decided it was the trending current colour, Perkins became extraordinarily rich. Perkins filed for a patent in August 1856, when he was still only 18. But apart from mauveine, it was a German chemical company Rider who saw the true potential of synthetic dyes and rapidly patented every other synthetic colour they could find. By 1900, nearly all patents for synthetic dyes were owned by German companies. The German stranglehold on colour finally got to young Perkins who relinquished his purple patent after the chemical company sent a host of patent spies, who represented themselves as respectable businessmen to convince Perkins to hand over his chemical mix.

I had never really considered the ruthless world of patents before, but as I contemplated patent espionage, parts of my lucid dream fitted into place. If Solley Weitzman aka Bill Wonder worked at Dapplewhites at the same time as my grandmother, hung around with her and then got thrown out for allegedly unusual sexual proclivities and then goes on to open a girdle factory in New York and produces the most hyped, albeit entirely unobtainable foundation underwear of the fifties could this all be about patents.

It now dawned on me in a purple haze epiphany, that what I actually needed was a patent specialist to see if, when and how the Silver corset and the Wonder girdle were connected. I became aware of a young guard snoozing on his stool. 'Do you know where I can find out about patents?' I asked.

He opened one eye, 'You need to go to the patent library, it's part of the British library. It's around the corner but you need to book an appointment,' he said and went back to snoozing.

Chapter 14
Universal Myths

That evening at 21.00 hours, having staked the school out for several hours to ensure no celebrities, students or hard faced business people were going to appear, I opened the back door and took the tradesman's lift up to the eighth floor and trip trapped through the office to the door that led to the balcony. The door was locked. I peered out the window trying to see whether the balcony showed signs of subsidence. I couldn't tell but something odd did catch my eye, a little further down the balcony was a small wall and the small wall appeared to be blowing smoke rings. A closer inspection was needed and I checked through the master keys. I was just about to open the door when I was distracted by what sounded like the glock glock mating call of the female swan.

I turned around slowly, trying to think why a randy swan would be pecking around on a Sunday evening. The swan didn't look as magnificent as it should and was standing on one bramble foot, leaning to one side at a precarious angle. Then the swan snorted, 'Oh sssSadie, sssSadie, what are you doing here late on a sssSunday? Are you planning your Monday morning work huddle?'

My heart plummeted, was I to be undone by a bird and a talking one at that? I looked at the swan again, judging from its quizzical right-angled stare, it was expecting an answer. I would have had problems explaining what I was doing in the school on a Sunday evening at the best of times and the Swan's disarrayed state and strangely familiar pensive glare was very unsettling.

The swan gave up on a reply and hissed some more sounds, 'Oh SSSadie, oh SSSadie, they have ssssacked me.'

I wasn't really sure why the school would employ a precariously balanced swan in the first place so remained mute.

The swan snorted bitterly, 'That "Don't Look Now" dwarf did it.'

It was my turn to gaze pensively at the swan that now seemed to want to discuss a disturbing 1970s classic film. Within the feathers, I could discern a human face and it was the face of Tanya the principal. I tried to make sense of the situation, had a dwarf turned her into a swan and then, judging by the disarray and wanton glocking, had some sort of sexual dealing with her. Was Tanya's new swan form divine retribution for her sin of hubris?

The Tanya swan creature started up again on the glocking and hissing and I wondered if "Don't look now", would happen again. I then had a more regular panicked thought. Would the Tanya creature be rational enough to want to know why I wasn't keeping to my suspension and become suspicious of my sneaking around in a rather slimming, burglar Bill outfit.

I breathed a sigh of relief. Tanya was the most self-obsessed person I had ever met and surely her new swan reincarnation would be double plus on the self-obsession. Could her total full immersion, self-obsession be used to my advantage? If I chatted to her about herself, maybe she wouldn't even think about me and if we spoke about whatever was troubling her... her sexually frustrated swan dwarf situation, then maybe she would forget about me altogether. In many ways, I was surprised she remembered my name, she didn't usually. I winged it, 'Yes Tanya, I have come in on a Sunday to plan tomorrow's early morning work huddle, but let's talk about you, as you're the most important person here.'

Tanya glocked less, 'Good,' she said. And I knew she was impervious to my suspension.

'Sharleen has sacked me,' she snorted. 'I leave on Friday.'

'No, that's so terrible and so unfair; tell me all about it, every little detail,' I lulled.

Her glocking which I realised was crying, calmed a little, 'Sharleen made me have a 360.'

'Really,' I gasped.

'She asked (well I suspect paid) other work colleagues, well underlings, to say honest without prejudice things about me,' she snivelled.

I winced for her. I have never really got my head around why any management consultants ever thought it was a good, nay productive idea, to ask poorly paid put upon workers to be honest about their horrible self-obsessed bosses without recrimination.

Tanya's swan continued her tale of management woe, 'My 360 was very good, but Sharleen fixated on the teeny-weeny bad points.' She stopped and honked in, 'Ssshe said my self-confidence was unjustified to the point of self-obsession and my power play lacked dddirection. And then,' choked Tanya, 'said she, 'my dress sense was outdated.'

'Gosh, what did you do?' I replied, hopefully displaying the correct emoji face.

'I lost my temper and and ....' Tanya stopped and I think she blushed.

'What did you do?' I asked gleefully.

'I went to the mock shop and got the tiny red plastic mac we were using for the Paddington Bear competition.'

'Yes,' I said enthralled.

She continued, 'And got a fake knife from the S and M window display.'

'Yes,' I was gripped.

'And I went to the library and got the film of *Don't look Now* and got IT to loop the end of the film, where the wizened female dwarf serial killer slashes John to death, starting from the bit where the serial killer shakes her head enigmatically as if to say you are wrong, up to his death.'

I was riveted, this sounded fabulous.

'I waited until Sharleen had gone out,' she continued, 'and then put the red plastic mac and the knife on her desk, and put the looped film scene of the slashing on her computer and stood outside her door.'

I genuinely crooned; it was the most brilliant shove your stupid job I have ever heard. 'Then what happened?' I squeaked.

'Well... then,' Tanya replied, blowing a feather off her face, 'she walked back into her office, sat down, and screamed, "You're fired..."'

'That's brilliant Tanya,' I said wide-eyed with genuine admiration. 'Did she understand the symbolism? That the figure in the red coat is both agonisingly vulnerable and deadly at the same time, just like her.'

'I'm not sure, she came out and told me that I am unstable and sick,' she replied and we both laughed heartily.

'But very imaginative,' I chortled.

'Maybe, but it went to the board and they were all very sorry but they said they would have to let me go,' she said swanfully.

'Talk about leaving in style though,' I added appreciatively.

'Thanks,' she swan-smiled at me.

'One thing though,' I asked my new better to die on your feet than live on your knees compadre.

'Yes.'

'Why are you dressed like a squashed swan?'

She ruffled triumphantly, 'Oh it's marvellous, isn't it. Rie Karaoke from his Monstrous Grotesque range, I haven't worn it at work yet, I wasn't sure if it was too dressy, what do you think?'

'Well, I can see why it's from the Grotesque range,' I replied, 'It's a nice colour but it's a bit, well, protruding and extended. Is the left side meant to be asymmetrical?'

'Yessss,' she said slowly in a "don't you know anything about fashion" way. 'It represents the processes of change as opposed to the classical form, which is monumental, static, closed, and sleek, at least that's what the label says.'

'Yes, I suppose it is far more connected to the real world,' I replied. 'Does it represent the first stage of mourning your decline, actually when did you say you are leaving?'

She began glocking again, 'My marching orders are next Friday, the board gave me the letter on Friday. I have five more days until I say adieu to my fashion dream.' She loomed closer to me and I thought she might peck me but she was instead being conspiratorial. 'They will have to carry me out,' she hissed and snapped her head in sharply.

I smiled. If I made it to Friday; I would so hide in the plant room and watch her being carried out. Tanya, I think, smiled back. I had never seen her smile so I couldn't be sure.

She snorted, 'I have decided to mark each day with a seminal outfit, tomorrow I will wear Carrie's prom dress to reflect my monstrous downfall.'

'Wow, are you doing before or after the pig blood scene?' I asked impressed.

'Before, but in hindsight I should go for after,' she agreed. 'I should start with terrifying.'

This surprised me, I thought her whole persona had been based on terrifying. I was rather excited about her five faces of the monstrous feminine though and decided to help her plan her dress downfall, 'What are you wearing the next day?'

'I'm not really sure,' she replied hesitantly.

'Well, ideally you need archaic mother, monstrous womb, vampire, witch possessed body, monstrous mother and castrator, may I suggest ending with castrator, that's good and ominous, let Sharleen think you'll be back for revenge.'

'Yes, she wouldn't want me to cut her balls off,' snorted Tanya and so did I.

'I think Monday counts as possessed body and archaic mother, so next you could do monstrous womb.'

We both looked at each other: what could she wear to represent that? And then for once we were of the same mind and said in unison, 'It will have to be a meat dress,' and we both laughed heartily again. Tanya and I having a witty metaphorical conversation about universal myths of the fallen woman, and how fashion can play in identifying these myths

121

in a modern social and cultural context, was perhaps one of the most unusual things about the last few days. I wondered if we could have been friends in a different life, this I wasn't sure about.

Tanya regained her officious self a little and said, 'I must go and order a meat dress, I'm sure the shop can drop one round for me, even though it's Sunday evening.'

Realising that our bonding moment was coming to an end, I too said, 'Yes, I must go and prepare some lessons for next week.'

Tanya rearranged her asymmetrical swan outfit and turned to go, she then stopped and said, 'Sadie, be careful. I do know exactly what is happening; you have been suspended and shouldn't be anywhere near the school. But as I've been sacked and we're getting on so well, I don't care.'

I nodded gratefully.

'And Sadie take this.' She handed me a small old-fashioned key. 'I'm giving you the key to the school's walk-in wardrobe, which is next to the shower room on the third floor. I think you should throw that bedraggled Chanel suit away now. I know it's vintage but it stinks, and oh one more thing Sadie, good luck. I hope you discover the truth.' She turned and waddled away.

I went to the third floor. As I walked past mannequin Betty Boop she definitely said, 'He couldn't take my boop-oop-a-doop away.' I looked at her and she stopped but when I started walking again, she said, 'Koko will save me.'

I climbed onto the Dora Duffy plinth and gazed at the corset pinned butterfly tight under the glass frame on the wall. As I climbed down, I slipped and knocked Dora Duffy and we both fell to the ground. Dora Duffy landed on top of me and her kissable lips zoomed in for a snog. As I wrestled Dora off me, she said her catchphrase, 'I've got an itch and I need it scratched,' but her bow shaped lips weren't moving and instead the voice seemed to be coming from the back of her mouth or even her head. I panicked as I tried to shake the automaton loose but her plastic spindly fingers were digging in, and her sexual innuendo catch-phrase kept repeating.

I finally managed to free myself from the possessed plastic mannequin and pushed her to the floor with all my might. She clattered face down and a small screw rolled from her body and her hair slowly slid to one side. Her corset remained unruffled though. She was still catch phrasing, even in her hairless death throes but the sound no longer sounded like words, it was more like the blaring sound that a Wookie makes.

Under her hair at the back of her head was a plastic panel, it opened easily. Inside were a sound synthesiser chip and a tiny amp and speaker. I righted Dora but couldn't stop her slurring catchphrase so I pulled out the synthesiser and disconnected the wires and she finally stopped her smutty rant. I started to put the disconnected chip back into her head when I noticed that someone had used a dusty pink matchbox previously, to stop her slurring. I pulled out the matchbox which had fallen to the bottom of her empty head and looked at it. It had a photograph of an American rodeo and the name Cowtown 1957.

I dusted myself down and pocketed the matchbox. I scanned the corridor for Tanya's walk-in wardrobe. There wasn't a door but I spotted a tiny keyhole in the panelling near the shower room. As I opened the door, a soft mellow light turned on and I stepped inside a TARDIS, a TARDIS filled with clothes. The wardrobe must have taken up almost all of the left side of the third floor and explained the size differentiation of the offices on the right compared to the left, which only had Bill's office and well, a hidden secret garden of clothing.

The wardrobe Narnia room was packed to the gunnels with designer clothes, shoes and bags. Two stories high with a ladder of wheels. The bottom shelves were full of thousands of designer shoes and there was a separate wall dedicated to designer bags ranging from pastel to black.

'Wow,' I gasped.

I was in heaven, the one drawback was that the clothes and shoes were several sizes too large and I looked a little like Minnie mouse, but I really didn't care.

I went home just as the sun was rising. I felt like I'd been clubbing all night. As I got off the tube at East Finchley, I bumped into Josue.

He looked purposeful, 'Hi Sadie, how are you? Why haven't you been to school recently, are you sick?' he asked intently.

I wasn't sure how to answer and nodded instead.

'You have missed some very strange things Sadie; I guess you know about Bill.'

I nodded.

'They arrested Jonathan and refused him bail.'

'Oh good… I mean oh dear. How is he?' I asked, trying to look surprised and sympathetic.

'I'm not sure Sadie; Alistair said he's a changed man …'

Josue shook his head anxiously, 'Sadie, do you have my keys? The set I lent you?'

'Yes I do. But not on me,' I lied, 'I will bring them back tomorrow, now I'm better.' I nodded in a mock reassuring way whilst wondering if I was ever coming back.

To change the subject, I enquired about Joya.

Josue shook his head, 'No one has heard from her. She has disappeared.'

'Probably saving the planet somewhere,' I nodded.

'Tanya has gone proper crazy. She and Sharleen fight all the time and I think Tanya has been sacked but I don't know for sure. This morning she had a wig of long flowing golden hair and a long white tunic and a large bouquet of red poppies and roses. I was too scared to talk to her but Maggie said she looked like the Pre-Raphaelite version of Lilith.'

'Who's Lilith?' I asked surprised. Tanya must have gone off script.

'I looked Lilith up, just in case she was a terrorist or something dangerous. Wiki said she was the first wife of Adam who demanded equality and wanted to have sex on top and Adam said no. Then she said, well I'm off then, I'd rather live by the sea than hang around with you in the Garden of Eden. Adam told God and he sent angels after her. But she still refused to come back. This, I think, must have been a blow for God and Adam. Adam was okay though, because to avoid any more arguments God created Adam a new wife called Eve, and well apart from the apple bit, it was much better,' Josue smirked.

I nodded in agreement, impressed by Tanya's understanding of irony.

'Sadie,' said Josue looking worried again, 'do you think Tanya is making a point with her outfits.'

'Yes, could be.'

'Sadie, how far do you think Tanya would go to make a point?'

'Are you asking me whether she would kill Bill?'

'Maybe.'

'Why do you think that?'

'You see the thing is, Tanya knew that I shouldn't bring you those boxes last week.'

'What, are you telling me she set me up?' I gasped in an indignant way.

'Maybe. One of the boxes was marked "strictly confidential for Bill's office only". It had tape all over it. I said no, I don't think this is a good idea but she was insistent.'

'So she knew I shouldn't open it. That opening it would get me into a whole shitload of trouble,' I choked. 'Why, what was she playing at? Deliberately getting me suspended, what for?'

'It's not just that though, is it,' continued Josue.

'What do you mean? It's been quite stressful for me,' I started to remonstrate.

'No Sadie, I mean is there a bigger picture. Why did she do that and has it got something to do with Bill's death?'

I shook my head; I really had no idea.

'Sadie,' Josue said dramatically, 'did you look in the box?'

Now I was worried, 'No,' I replied unconvincingly.

'Sadie,' Josue repeated with as much menace as he could muster, 'did you look in the box?'

'Well I must be off; I'm er, meeting someone in Warren Street,' I lied to avoid answering.

'That's a coincidence, I'm going to school, we can travel together.' He smiled in a "game on" way.

My heart sank, would Josue grill me all along the Northern line. To circumvent any incriminating information spilling out, I started on a tale about my Bubbe.

'I remembered the buying trips I would go on with my grandmother,' I began, 'We would head down Mortimer Street where the wholesale agents had their clothing outlets. Global sweatshops were just a dream back then and clothes were sourced from UK sweatshops, many in and around Brick lane or the Midlands.'

Josue nodded in a disinterested way, 'Yes, but can we talk about ....'

I ignored him and continued in a Mags Twill bouldering way, 'The perfect old-school model of buying, as taught to me by Bubbe is this. March around your opponent's wholesale domain, looking disappointed and saddened by the quality, cut and style of the goods. Try and fetter, I have wasted my time vibes. Feeling the material, tutting and sighing works well, muttering disparaging comments helps, and a particularly effective weapon I now realise, is an almost cute chubby slightly overwhelmed child, who you have briefed on the intricacies of the end game for several days beforehand.'

'Sadie, can we talk about the box...'

'Bubbe would mutter things to me and then I had to act accordingly and make innocent wide-eyed comments such as, 'Really grandma the stitching has come loose on this dress already and the zip doesn't work.' I laughed heartily and noticed that most of the carriage was now listening to me. I felt like Scheherazade.

Josue nodded in an uninterested way.

'Prices would now turn to percentages and figures would fly around at an alarming pace, take 10% off that figure and add 15 more dresses size 14, add 12.5%, and I will throw in 5 cardigans etc.' I rabbited on nervously.

'Sadie, can we talk about the incident now,' blurted Josue.

Several passengers hushed him.

'No one had a calculator and all calculations were done in your head,' I continued and some of the older passenger's nodded in agreement.

'Sometimes I was allowed to innocently chime a ridiculously low figure, and if accepted, it was dinner at the Post Office Tower that evening,' I added.

'Yes, that's how it was done, in the old days,' said an elderly man dressed in a single-breasted Monaco wool suit. A few other passengers clapped and one dropped a fiver into my haut tote.

'The revolving one at the top of the tower?' asked another passenger.

'Yes, I remember feeling vaguely sick throughout dinner.'

'Yes, I think lots of people did, that's why it closed.'

'They also didn't serve my favourite meal, beans on toast,' I laughed.

'Sadie, I want to ask you something.'

'Ok,' I replied in a guarded way.

'Do you think Bill just fell off the balcony?'

I noticed the rest of the carriage was now utterly gripped.

'I really don't know.'

'Sadie, can I tell you something in confidence?'

I shook my head; I really couldn't cope with any more secrets but Josue told me anyway.

'The railings on the balcony are loose, I do not know why. I checked them the other day and they wobble. They didn't used to, so I don't know how this happened.'

I felt sorry for Josue and as he has always been a good guy. I revealed one of my more general knowledge snippets of Intel. 'Subsidence,' I replied.

'What do you mean?'

'The Underground boring tunnel is causing subsidence issues around Tottenham Court Rd. I read about it in a newsletter whilst having coffee at the House of Charity coffee shop.'

'Do you think Bill just tripped over them? Can I be sacked for this?'

'Nnoooo,' I replied, hopefully managing to sound reassuring whilst thinking these were exactly my thoughts. As Josue looked so anxious, I added, 'But Josue, the railing is quite high and Bill was very short, he would have had to be standing on something to just tumble over.'

'Arr Si, Si of course. Thank you, Sadie, you always add balance, I will stop thinking I am to blame now. I think you should come back to school soon, your balance is missing.'

'Really, did I add balance?' I replied. I had never thought of myself in that way, more indecisive, lacking in self-confidence, mildly hysterical.

It's funny how others see you.

'Remember my keys,' Josue shouted after me as I got off for my non-existent appointment.

Chapter 15
Mashers and Other Deviations

Kimberley called early next morning, well around 9 am which is early for my new lacking employment state.

'Sadie, Sadie I have discovered some really interesting stuff,' she gushed, 'and I've booked us a table at the Rose Garden, see you later and don't worry, I'm paying. I have more cash than I know what to do with.'

I sent Kimberley an emoji smiley face and thumbs up. *Oh the young*, I mused, with their easy to understand accessible non-grammatical language.

I pulled out the Chanel and was hit by the smell. I held her up to the light and finally had to admit that 60 years of hanging elegantly around my grandmother and then me was finally beginning to show.

'I guess it's about time I put you out to pasture my old friend,' I sighed resignedly.

Aware that I couldn't meet Kimberley at one of the most expensive hotel restaurants in London in one of my "it's so cheap I may as well buy it" outfits, or even one of my "fake designer try and fit in at the fashion school" numbers. I rummaged around in the large portmanteau my grandmother had sent me when she moved to the nursing home. As I worked my way through the Schaips and the Balmains and Jacques Fath, I thought of Bubbe meticulously measuring and re-measuring her clients to ensure she produced the perfect corset for their body size, and the exhilaration she must have felt when she finished her piece de resistance, "the Silver corset" with its nine diagonal sections which could be adjusted to form the perfect nonpareil body armour. I pulled out a Yves Saint Laurent Le Smoking tuxedo dinner jacket, in black grain de poudre wool with a satin side stripe and also found a black bow tie and a wide cummerbund. I have to admit I did have to add a pair of jeggings and a £4 T-shirt.

Kimberley looked covert and I suspect sexually alluring, in big sunglasses and a Sophia Loren red patent raincoat. She was lounging in the fake, feel at home living room area. I have trouble with this concept. If I'm going to be wined and dined at an exorbitant cost, I would prefer not to be reminded of real-life domestic interiors.

Kimberley waved me over whilst ordering, 'Three bottles of 2006 Perrier-Jouët, Belle Époque and a canapé selection please.'

'So how are you Sadie?' she asked enthusiastically, 'How's the corset hunt going?'

'I'm good, thanks. Not sure about the corset hunt, I seem to be going round in circles. I'm going to Patlib tomorrow.'

'Is that a new type of cosmetic surgery? Should I get one?'

'Haha no… It's the patent library at the British museum. I'm going to check out the patent situation.'

'Good idea but wait until you hear what I've found out.'

'Okay go for it.' I said hitting the bubbly.

'Right, so where do I start? … With Solley Weitzman I guess.'

'You found him?' I exclaimed.

'Yep. You're quite open-minded about what granny did aren't you?' she asked tentatively.

'Consider me unshockable,' I replied.

Kimberley produced an old ledger which she had somehow compressed into her John Ford mini diamond disco backpack. 'I went through Dapplewhites' old staff reports and found a Solley Weitzman in the staff ledger from 1955. He worked for a Maud Wilson who sounded like an officious battle axe.'

'Yes, I've heard about her too, very good at her job apparently.'

'She kept very comprehensive files on all the staff that worked for her. Solley was at Daps for 19 months and according to Maud, would have got sacked if he hadn't chosen to leave.'

'Why?'

'Read this.' Kimberley pointed to a neatly written section with the heading Solley Weitzman. *3rd assistant merchandiser menswear.*

10 December 1956: 'Solley Weitzman shows promise. He demonstrates business acumen and a solid grasp of retail commerce. Spends too much time in the lingerie section and is always very keen to speak to one of our suppliers, Bobena Silver. He has been warned about this. Solley has passed his probationary term. Aims and objectives for the coming year are appearance, customer service and to increase sales.'

'It's like HR from the grave,' I muttered.

'Read on,' urged Kimberley.

January 2nd 1957: There has been a report that Solley Weitzman is indulging in odd sexual proclivities. This is yet to be substantiated.

January 20th 1957: There has been a further report of Solley Weitzman indulging in odd sexual proclivities. I have asked Murray Treadwell, the new head of security, to investigate.

February 12th 1957: Mr Treadwell reports that Solly Weitzman acted in a morally inappropriate way. Mr Treadwell and I will question him about this matter tomorrow morning just after the weekly sales report.

February 13TH 1957: Mr Treadwell and I questioned Solley Weitzman for 2 hours. Mr Treadwell used a technique he had mastered in Malaysia as part of his army interrogation training and approached the interview with military thoroughness. At first Solley Weitzman denied any wrongdoing. Mr Treadwell became frustrated by the lack of progress and produced one of the fox handle riding sticks (which sell so well in men's toiletries) and pinned Solley Weitzman to a Barolo desk retailing at £24.99. I took Mr

Treadwell aside and made it clear that Dapplewhites would not condone physical damage. He reluctantly changed track and used an approach known as Step 2 in which blame is shifted away from the suspect to another person or set of circumstances that have prompted the suspect to commit the crime. To this end Mr Treadwell told Solley Weitzman that he had already interviewed Bobena Silver and he knew all about their arrangement. Solley Weitzman looked shocked and saddened by this and said 'But we could have made a fortune. Why has she betrayed me?' Mr Treadwell replied, 'everyone has a price and besides, she's a Jew, they will say anything to save their own necks.' It was suggested to Solley that if he left immediately and never worked in retail in the UK again, the store wouldn't press charges. Solley agreed to this and was escorted out. Although I had some reservations about Mr Treadwell's interrogation methods. The end result was satisfactory.

'Wow, so what was Solley doing? The old guy "Oswald" I met at the funeral said he thought Solley was a masher.'

'What's a masher?' asked Kimberly typing it on her phone.

'I had to look it up; it's an old-fashioned word for a sexual molester.'

'What like someone who hangs around lingerie departments giving women a quick grope?'

'Yes, or possibly worse.'

'Would explain why he got kicked out of Daps.'

'Sadie, do you think he was doing masher stuff with your grandmother?'

'I hope not, but if he had tried, she would have definitely whacked him with a fox handle riding stick. No, I don't think that's what they were up to. But it could explain why he would move to New York and change his name to Bill Wonder.'

'And if he worked at Daps and hung around with your grandmother, he would have learnt about corsets.'

'And if he thought Bobena had betrayed him, he could well have stolen her new prototype corset.'

'The corset that Mr Dapplewhite, the elder's listed in his ledger.'

'Yes.'

'So,' burped Kimberley, 'just to get all this clear, we now think Solley Weitzman was a masher and when he got caught, he thought he had been betrayed by his older woman friend Bobena Silver, so he stole Bobena's new innovative corset design and moved to America, changed his name to Bill Wonder and somehow found enough money to set up a large factory where he mass produced the Wonder Girdle and became a billionaire.'

'Yes,' I replied hesitantly.

'A few things come to mind, firstly was he a masher and does that matter?'

'I think he must have been some sort of masher, otherwise why would there have been reports of his masher proclivities and why did he go quietly?'

'Errrr what sort of masher was he?'

'Is that relevant?'

'Hell yes, I sell my body to older men for large sums of money, I therefore live outside social norms.' Kimberley said indignantly whilst ordering more champagne.

'You mean social norms change and what might have been considered deviance in 1957 isn't now?'

'Yes, it's a shame they didn't have surveillance cameras back then.'

'I'm not sure his particular masher proclivities are relevant in this case, be they acceptable now or not. The point is, they resulted in him being kicked out of Dapplewhites and he had a misguided grudge against my grandmother.'

'But if whatever he was doing was considered acceptable then, he wouldn't have been kicked out and the whole chain of events that followed might not have happened.'

'Yep maybe, but I'm having enough trouble trying to get my head around what happened between him and my grandmother and I can't really get my head around Zen-like morality and ethics at the moment.'

'I wonder if Solley (or Bill) ever found out that Treadwell made up the stuff about her reporting his masher proclivities.'

'I wonder how far a masher would go for revenge.'

'If he was or wasn't a masher, he would still have been angry.'

'Angry enough to steal a corset?'

'Well yes.'

'What it does not explain is why my grandmother kept quiet about it all.'

'And it doesn't explain why your grandmother stopped making corsets and moved to Devon.'

'Were they connected, the profession she loved and the move to Devon?'

'No, I don't think so; it was just a place to lie low.'

'And I suppose we now have to wonder, why was she lying low if he was the masher?'

'Because he was blackmailing or had something on her,' I suggested.

'But he was the masher or maybe they were like mashers together, mashers in crime, that's happens you know when you get two like-minded psychos together, they egg each other on,' Kimberley gushed, 'And then he got caught and she didn't and their only code of morality was not to grass on each other.'

I downed a glass of champagne in one and wondered whether Kimberley could be right. Had Bill and my Bubbe been up to no good, something unpleasant and criminal? Pornography came to mind but judging by the photographs in the album, that didn't seem likely. Could it be drugs or murder, the modern-day catalyst for every crime box set I watch? Had Bubbe and Bill been operating as 1950s drug lords operating out of a turn of the century department store, using lingerie as a cover? I guess it could be possible. If so, was I inadvertently exposing things from the past that my grandmother had spent the last fifty years covering up. I downed another glass or two and tried to stitch it all together.

'Oh my goodness,' Kimberley giggled, 'I forget the other thing. Right, the other thing is this. Before I found Solley, I

134

tried to find a Wonder Girdle. I know they stopped making them ages ago, but in the 1950s 1 in 3 women had one.' She leaned in theatrically, 'But you know, I couldn't find a Wonder girdle anywhere. I searched all the online vintage corset shops, went to corset auctions, even went to the VA clothing collection and no-one had one.'

'I know, no one can find one. Judith Trouser couldn't find one either.'

'See what I mean,' exclaimed Kimberley. 'Finally I went on the deep web and found a corset collector in Oklahoma. He said he had been searching for a Wonder girdle for years, and then, by chance, he came across a much damaged one, well one with lots of bullet holes in a Preppers store in Phoenix Arizona. He said it was the hardest girdle he had ever tracked down, which is really strange given its alleged popularity,' Kimberley said munching on a Calamansi jelly roe canape. 'And now it gets even stranger. The corset collector said when he finally got his hands on the Wonder girdle and tried it on; it didn't suck his figure in at all.'

'Really?'

'Yes, he was so upset he sent the corset off to a lab to try and discover the secret material used in it. When the report came back, the secret material was nitrile rubber.'

'Okay, is that bad for your skin or the environment or something?'

'Not bad, just odd. It belongs to a family of unsaturated copolymers and various butadiene monomers and is incredibly strong. It can withstand temperatures from −40 to 108 °C and is generally resistant to oil, fuel, and other chemicals. It is used for protective clothing in the nuclear industry.'

'Ummm, I didn't understand a lot of the compound words,' I said, aware that I was now swimmingly drunk.

'Sorry, I forgot I have a degree in biochemistry,' Kimberley said. 'But the thing about nitrile rubber is this, because it's the only form of synthetic rubber which is resistant to oil, fuel, and other chemicals, it is very inflexible. It would be the worst type of rubber to make a girdle designed to suck you in. You could make a very good inflexible shaped body suit out of it, but it would be almost impossible to clinch.'

'So you would have a good chance of surviving an apocalypse in it, but one of the few things you couldn't do with it is make a flexible girdle that sucks your figure into a curvy silhouette.'

'Correct.'

'Was it actually a Wonder girdle, not a copy?'

'I think so.'

'But, but why would Bill use it to make a girdle?'

'Exactly.'

'Please tell me you have an answer,' I replied as a desperate drunken fugue started to encase my thoughts.

'I have a few theories, well to be fair Mr Dapplewhite had a suspicion, and the corset collector in Oklahoma had a theory.'

'Tell me,' I sighed as mannequins dressed in shocking pink corsets danced around my frontal cortex.

'Suspicion one; was the Wonder girdle actually an elaborate marketing ploy? You have never seen one or known anyone who owned one. I couldn't find one and Mr Dapplewhite said when Dapplewhites looked into stocking it, the factory in New York never responded to their requests. Did the Wonder girdle actually exist or was it all marketing hype?'

'Actually that's what Judith Trouser thinks. But why go to all that trouble, building a factory, making a film, sending out brochures and catalogues?'

'Exactly, why go to all that trouble?' confirmed Kimberley.

'You have an answer, don't you?'

'Well, again it's only a theory, but the corset collector said the girdle was made with a compound mix that was patented by IG Rosa.'

'IG Rosa, the giant pharmaceutical company in Germany who owned most of the world's synthetic dyes?'

'Yes.'

'Is this a conspiracy theory?'

'Of course it is, the corset collector was a prepper.'

'Hit me with it,' I replied spilling champagne down my chin.

'IG Rosa owned most of the world's synthetic materials including the basic compounds for cosmetics, fertilisers, pesticides, medicines and chemicals for the film and photo industries.'

'Wow. Go on,' I rallied.

'They were the first to invent and patent butadiene, which is the key ingredient of nitrile rubber.'

'Okay, but what's the corset connection?'

'The corset collector thinks it's because IG Rosa ran camouflage companies around the world.'

'To hide what is actually going on?'

'Yes.'

'Wow, IG Rosa was a particularly evil multinational, even by multinational standards. They bankrolled the Nazi party and built Auschwitz and as we all know, tested out many of their inventions on the concentration camp prisoners.'

'So could the Wonder Company be a camouflage company for IG Rosa's latest banned experiments?'

'It would make a very feasible camouflage company, particularly if they were developing new material compounds.'

'Like different types of rubber which they were allegedly using to make girdles.'

'Exactly, maybe they were trying to develop some new type of military weapon, that's where the money is nowadays.'

'Like highly sophisticated body armour?'

'Yes.'

'Like Terminator.'

'And that would explain why the Wonder girdle is impossible to track down because they only made a few samples.'

'Yep,' giggled Kimberley, pouring more champagne.

'Maybe the FBI or the KGB killed Bill?'

'Or British Intelligence, they are usually behind arms dealing,' agreed Kimberley.

'You could be right…' I began, but Kimberley's phone beeped and beeped again very shortly afterwards.

'Arr sorry Sadie, will have to leave you in the middle of all this girdle cloak and dagger. I have an appointment with an old sailor, well a retired captain of a ship. He wants me to tap dance.

Kimberley laughed. 'You should have given us assignments like this; it's so much more fun.'

I smiled.

'Are you free on Friday? I'm doing some market research. Think you will like it. Good luck at catnip.'

'Patlib… thanks, will text if I find anything,' I waved as she tap-danced out just missing the waiter.

On a whim I decided to visit my grandmother. I just about made it to Paddington and then fell asleep on the train to Bournemouth; fortunately a kindly soul tapped me awake just as the train pulled in. Getting pissed during the day is never a good idea. Before visiting my grandmother, I straightened my bowtie and tucked in my shirt, in the nursing home toilet. I noticed that the hem on my £4 fast fashion jeggings had come loose. I could sew that up I thought but then decided it would be less hassle to just throw them away and buy a new pair.

Bubbe was awake and even looked excited to see me. 'Sadie, Sadie how are you bubula,' she said pinching my cheeks. And then said, 'Sadie you're drunk,' in an accusatory way.

'I had a few glasses of champagne,' I replied trying my best to not look drunk.

'Your tie is askew; your hem is loose and your waistcoat is missing a button.'

'I know Bubbe, I'm sorry but I have some important things I want to discuss with you.'

'I'm not sure I want to talk to someone who is drunk.'

'Please Bubbe; I have Bill's photograph album and the account ledgers for Dapplewhites. I'm just not sure what they mean,' I said thrusting the open photographic album on her lap.

Bubbe looked down, 'Sadie you have arrived drunk and are now making me look at naked young man.'

I noticed the nursing home staff moving in nervously.

'But wait there's Anai,' Bubbe said pointing to an innocuous flabby young man.

'Actually Bubbe, there is a photograph of you and Anai but it's a bit further on,' I said hastily turning the pages over.

'But I just saw the photograph Sadie,' she remonstrated trying to turn the pages back.

'No it's further on. She is standing next to you outside your Silver workshop …'

'You're very difficult when you're drunk, rather like your father. He was an awkward young man, had the devil in him,' She growled, forcefully turning the pages back.

'I'm not that drunk Bubbe, please focus,' I shouted in frustration but something had shut down in Bubbe. Her lips had pursed and she crossed her arms.

'I will have to ask you to leave now,' one of the bigger staff members said and I was very thoroughly escorted out of the nursing home.

It wasn't until I got home and made a strong black coffee that I realised I had left the photograph album and the ledger at Bubbe's nursing home.

Chapter 16
Death to Copyists

'As Madeleine Vionnet said, "death to copyists"...' I muttered while smoothing down my, well my grandmother's, Andre Courreges ready-to-wear red and white Moon Girl A line dress with matching flat white go-go boots as I waited at the desk in the Business and IP Centre at the British Library.

'You don't walk through life anymore, you run,' a stunning paper-thin blonde said as she stared at me with an exacting look.

'Clothes must be able to move too,' I replied

'Andre Courreges started his career as an engineer. You can always see that level of practicality in his cheerful clean lines.'

'Yes, I agree,' I nodded enthusiastically.

'Did you choose the outfit because you thought it would go with the clear plastic bag?'

'No, I had completely forgotten that you had to dispense of all your worldly goods in the cloak room. I haven't been here for a while.'

'That is interesting, very interesting.'

'Is it.'

' I always like to, what do you English say, 'weigh up' the people who do research in the B and IP centre. You don't quite fit. I'm Marta, your patent information specialist,' she said smiling suspiciously.

I wasn't entirely sure how to answer this particularly as Marta had clearly blown all my preconceptions of what a librarian should look like. 'Hi, I'm Sadie Silver. I'm looking for a patent for a corset my grandmother Bobena Silver made in the fifties. I emailed you about it.'

'Yes, yes, yes I have read your email. I would like to say I am very excited by this patent hunt,' she said in a very non-excited way. 'It brings into play all the things I like best, underwear, fashion and,' she whispered conspiratorially, 'given the sudden interest, I'm guessing some sort of rightful ownership dispute.'

'Has there been a sudden interest?' I queried.

Marta ignored me and instead rather hurriedly pointed at a computer and said, 'If you go into Escapenet you should find what you are looking for in Basement 1, press 5318-25.' She then gave a flounce, a hair flick and cat walked down the library.

I think my hopelessly confused countenance pulled at something as she stopped, pirouetted, pouted and turned and gave me a resigned look and glided back to the computer. After much elegant typing and some tutting she beckoned me over.

'This is what you are looking for,' she smouldered and then muttered, 'The English are a lazy nation.'

'Is it? Thanks,' I replied nervously.

Marta pointed to the database reference. It said, 'A five panel corset with zipper and steel casing registered by the Silver Workshop in 1956.'

'I'm guessing this is it,' she asked as she laconically stretched her lithe willowy limbs.

I nodded.

'So it was patented correctly and in an ideal world, if someone tried to copy it, your grandmother could have stopped it but you will find there is often a but with a patent.' She stopped suddenly and I think she laughed.

'Really' I replied anxiously.

'Patent history reads like a database tapestry of power play and misplaced ideology,' she exhaled and stretched her leggy limbs further. 'And you know this is why I love this job, it always comes down to the fine detail, the weft threads. They always build up the bigger picture. I used to be a lingerie model but it was so stark and detail-less,' she pouted.

'I'm not surprised,' I burbled.

'The design drawings were accepted, the shape, configuration and how the parts were fitted together are documented here.' Martha said pointing to a hand drawn illustration of a hidden zipper inserted into the back of a corset rather than the traditional flange and hooks. Next to it were several smaller illustrations of the nine separate pieces with detailed handwritten information on how they fitted together. The ninth piece looked a bit odd and didn't quite seem to fit but as Marta had started talking again, I focused on her.

'Look,' she continued, 'we have a copy of the original letter from the solicitor. A, Mr Hans Kotchemschi, Berners Street, W1. It's dated 9th September 1955. It is registered correctly. Would you like a copy? I can print one out.'

'Yes please.'

'Are you all checking it's all correct before you remake it? I think you're right, you can't beat a good corset, these spanks don't really work,' Marta said plucking her minuscule waist.

Marta handed me the photocopy absentmindedly.

'Thanks, Marta,'

Marta was busy tapping lost in patent history. 'This is fascinating,' she dazzled. 'I think we have a 7624337 and a 9604. Wow, this is marvellous?' she shimmered whilst shaking her lustrous perfectly highlighted blonde hair and I think tiny stars fell from it.

I looked at the patent of my grandmother's corset and then took out the torn page from 'Wife' with the Wonder girdle illustrations of woman with vacuum, woman hanging out washing, woman bending over. The corset and the girdle both had nine long spiral panels which flattered the body and smoothed any dispersed flab under its petal like panels to create a perfect hourglass figure. They both had a discrete hidden zipper. They both had a bullet shaped top line ending in, what had been described in fashion myths as 'perfect cherry orbs'. And although it was unclear in the 'Wife' illustrations my grandmother's meticulous drawings indicated that the pointed preformed conical stitching allowed for the foam rubber falsies to be inserted from the side. Again although unspecified in "Wife", Bubbe had written notes about a new material known as Fibre J, a rayon polymer which was just about to be released to market. And they were of course both a shocking pink trimmed with black braiding.

Marta noticed me comparing the patent with the illustrations, 'You're not allowed to bring in additional papers.' she said haughtily.

'Sorry,' I replied, 'I'm just comparing my grandmother's Silver corset with Bill Wonders girdle.'

'What?' screamed Marta in a not so beautiful way.

'Yes sorry I know I shouldn't have brought the extra paper in.' I began feeling unnerved by Marta's contorted face.

'Wait' Marta said curtly and looked a little horsey. 'Are you talking about the origins of the Wonder girdle and the Wonder Empire?'

'Yes.'

'So you are saying that the Silver corset becomes the Wonder girdle?'

'Well I wasn't sure but now I've seen my grandmother's patent design and the illustrations from "Wife", I think they are the same design.'

'But, but that's actually significant, that's more significant than,' Marta breathed in and twinkled, 'Reactionary Modernism.'

'Is it?' I replied bemused.

'Yes, we are talking about the Wonder Empire, the living breathing black hole of capitalism. I had no idea and more to the point, what I can do to help; I'm guessing your aim is to destroy it,' Marta in an eager to help, cutesy and bloodthirsty way.

Marta removed the two papers from my hands and moved her large blue eyes from side to side and managed to open them a little wider each time. Then she said with finality. 'And so it begins, and so finally I sense it will happen, yes it is always the small details that topple the biggest empires.'

'And so do you think they are the same design?' I asked.

'Yes, Yes I do.'

'Do you know anything about patent laws, like can you sue someone for a historical patent infringement?'

'Yes and no.'

'What does that mean?'

'Yes, you can but you have to bring the case within seven years of the alleged infringement.'

'So, the late fifties don't count then.'

'No.'

'Really,' I sighed as all my pre-existing half-cocked theories and the prospect of punitive damages instantly fell apart.

'So I can't really use this information.'

'Not in a court of law. No. But there are other ways to bring down an Empire. But first, tell me was your grandmother a bit slow, a bit stupid. Maybe could we say a distracted artisan. '

'Not then, she's a bit random now, but no, she was a very good business woman then.'

'Did she speak English?'

'Yes, well Yinglish.'

And so, I ask the question, 'Why didn't she do anything at the time? When Bill Wonder was making his millions with your grandmother's girdle.'

'I really don't know.'

'That is the question that now needs to be answered.'

`I know I have tried to speak to her about it.'

'You know, I used to model for Best Girl catalogues. It was my first job in London. I was sixteen and had come from a village in the Czech Republic. I was so excited. But then I had a haircut and Best Girl wouldn't pay me because they said contractually, I wasn't allowed to cut my hair without their permission. I was penniless and miserable and scared. If I had enough money to take the coach back to Litvinov, I would have,' Marta said with deadpan angry vitriol.

'I'm very sorry to hear that,' I replied.

'You know what I will do now,' Marta said with a determined pout.

I shook my head.

'I will ask my fast streaming friends about other ways of bringing down the empire. May I use your patent information?'

'I guess so.'

'I finish what I start. I believe in business terms this makes me a shipper,' Marta said as revenge game plans furrowed her beautiful brow.

'Marta, who else has been checking out the patent,. Has someone from Bill Wonder's office asked about the Silver corset?'

Marta screwed up her eyes and growled and then went back to tapping. 'Here, I shouldn't give this list to you, data protection is a new very strict and clever way of enforcing disinformation or is that lack of information but if it helps to bring down the Empire so be it,' she said surreptitiously passing me a printout whilst pointing to the security cameras and nodding her head to indicate I shouldn't open the print out in the library.

'What do you intend to do with this information, Sadie?'

'I'm really not sure now. You know Bill Wonder is dead now?'

'Yes, I heard. It's a shame; I would have liked to have done it myself.'

'Yes, he seemed to have that effect on people.'

'Sadie,' she said with steely resolve as she sort of kneeled down in a knightly way, 'I will do all I can to help you bring shame on the Empire.'

'Thanks. Do I need a sword or something to knight you with?' I added.

Marta looked puzzled, 'I would also suggest the National Archives because the beginning of this story is often the crux, the catalyst but it's not really my field and one should never speculate without a fact.'

'So the beginning of my story will be the last thing I unfold,' I mused.

'It's often the way with history; you start at the end and end up at the beginning.'

'And once again thank you for helping. I was being a bit ungracious and well, British a minute ago.'

'No matter. I have come to understand that what is perceived as rudeness in my country is what the English call sarcasm, or only having a laugh.'

'Yes, you're probably right.'

'I promise to contact you the moment I find any relevant information,`` Marta said, saluting me as I left.

I waited until I was sitting on the tube before opening the printout. It was a list of people who had requested information about the Silver Corset – Miyake Hayat, Tanya Robinson, Joya Anderson and of course Sadie Silver.

'Tanya,' I gasped, 'Joya, Hayat Miyake,' I squeaked and I felt even more confused than before.

When I got home, my front door seemed to sense I was beat and refused to open. I eventually managed to shove it open and discovered a heavy brown envelope was impeding my entry. It had the red triangle and the empty platitude "Ensuring you will be the best you can be" Fashion school logo on it. I was going to ignore it, maybe just leave it behind the door and run the door over it every time I entered but I noticed the words, "no longer suspended" materialising from a torn corner so I opened it.

The letter was from Gita in HR and as long as I signed all the relevant non-disclosure forms, I was no longer suspended and my return was scheduled for Monday. The news didn't make me feel happy or grateful or relieved, it made me feel nervous. It wasn't just the sort of feeling one felt about returning to work after a long absence, it was deeper and more untethered. It felt more like I was no longer morally or justifiably able to engage with the discourse of fast fashion. I remembered one of Bill's sayings, 'If you wake up in the morning and don't like what you do, do something else.' I certainly needed to do something else and was about to throw the envelope in the bin and maybe ring Gita and say, 'shove your rotten job up your ...' when it dawned on me that I didn't have a plan B and the rent was due on the 5th and I resigned myself to 8.50 am start on Monday with my pre-prepared PowerPoint on the history of Charles Worth and the beginnings of the designer label. It also occurred to me that it must be much easier to suddenly "do something else" if you are a multi-millionaire.

I put the signed disclosure forms on top of the cocktail cabinet next to the photo of Bobena and paced my living room trying to arrange my thoughts in some sort of logical order. As I paced, I glanced over at the photograph of Bubbe.

'Why didn't you ever make a claim against the Wonder Girdle and why did you run off to Devon?' I asked the photograph wondering why I had never asked for these details before? Was I remiss in my granddaughter duties? I couldn't really remember the nuances of the conversations we had. I guess one doesn't. And I also guessed I didn't know then what I know now.

Did Bill offer Bubbe a golden handshake, I pondered but if that was the case, why did she bear such a grudge and why didn't she tell me. She loved telling me stories about how she had come out on top despite adversity. Had it all been resolved in a financially satisfactory way and did Bubbe just hate Bill because he was an annoying dickhead. He certainly was one when he became a billionaire so I guess he probably was one beforehand but my grandmother wasn't scared of domineering unpleasant men, she used to enjoy a verbal dispute. If an angry husband came into the shop to complain about the deeply impractical clothes Bubbe had convinced a harangued farmer's wife into buying knowing full there would never be an occasion in which a Jean Louis mustard crepe evening dress with rhinestone trim could be worn with wellington boots, Bubbe would seamlessly turn it around and often the irate husband would leave having bought several other accessories. No, it was something else, something that I was missing. But I was no closer to figuring it out now than when I first hid in the plant room.

As I mused, I caught Bubbe's intense Kodachrome gaze and she seemed to be saying, 'What are you doing now? There's work to be done.'

'I know Bubbe,' I replied, 'but I'm all out of options and come Monday, I will have to settle down to my predestined role as a provider, facilitator, tutor of fashion history to young fashionistas eager to join the exciting, glamourous, underpaid and ruthless world of fast fashion.'

'Grrrrr,' Bubbe said, 'but until then I suggest you get to it.'

'You're right Bubbe, and the very least I can do is go get your corset,' I answered.

I think my grandmother's photograph was now shouting something like, 'What, what do I need a corset for? I'm 94 and live in a nursing home.'

Chapter 17
Conspicuous Consumption

I galloped up the escalator at Tottenham Court Road and bumped into Trixie. She was wearing a pale blue Bashion Boiler suit which did suit her.

'Sadie,' she gasped surprised.

'Trixie, how are you? I love what you're wearing,' I replied.

'It's compulsory.'

'What the boiler suit?' I asked in amazement.

'Yes, Sharleen's orders. Apparently, our own clothes were infringing new health and safety rules.'

'I'm coming back on Monday,' I announced. 'Will I have to wear one?'

'I should think so.'

'Do you get to choose the colour?'

'No, colour is no longer a choice.'

'Really, it all sounds a bit Maoist.'

'Maybe,' Trixie replied in a hushed tone.

'See you at school or maybe the Princess Lisa for lunch?'

'We tend to meet in that damp cellar bar "Worcester and Hollingsworth" nowadays as Sharleen doesn't like us communicating after work.' she answered with finite acceptance.

'I'm meeting Kimberley in 20 minutes.'

'Kimberley Clark, I hear she is running a brothel, I was thinking about seeing if she has any openings.'

'She has some sort of test you have to pass.'

'What's in it?'

'I don't know. She said I wouldn't pass it.'

'Do you feel slighted?'

'Not really, I recognise there are many things I can't do, I guess prostitution is one of them.'

'I must go now, Sadie, my 13-minute lunch break is up.'

'Nice to see you again,' I replied as Trixie hurried off in an agitated state.

Kimberley was dancing with excitement when I met her. 'You're going to love what we are going to do today,' she chirped, 'try and guess. Go on... I'll give you three guesses,' she said as she pirouetted around me.

'I have no idea, you said something about market research,' I replied in a grouchy way.

'Just you wait.'

We had stopped at the junction of Oxford Street and Tottenham Court Road next to Centre Point. Kimberley produced an old-fashioned deadlock key.

'Only a few people have one of these,' she said triumphantly steering me under the scaffolding to a trompe l'oeil shop front. As she pressed the key on the pretend door, the fake shop front rolled up and we were greeted by a three-dimensional facsimile of Seurat's "Sunday Afternoon on the Grand Jatte".

'Where are we?' I gasped in wonderment.

'It's a new retail concept Miyake Industries are trailing. It's called a shopping biosphere.'

We were directed to changing rooms and asked to change into Bashion suits, whilst mini solar panels like devices were attached around our heads.

'What's going to happen now?' I hissed.

Before Kimberley had time to reply, we were herded out and told to sit on park benches for the introduction to our market research session.

A peppy young woman in a mauveine Bashion boiler suit began, 'Thank you for coming today. We hope you enjoy the market research experience and provide us with relevant feedback. I'm sure you read the literature about today when you signed the consent form.'

151

I glared at Kimberley and she mouthed "sorry", as she indicated she had signed for me.

'Miyake Industries believe that a new shopping paradigm is required and to that end are trialling several new shopping biosphere concepts. Today's concept as you have probably guessed is a pointillist interpretation of a sunny afternoon in Paris. Circa 1884. As you would have read, we have moved away from the old-fashioned concept of browsing goods and then paying for them in a physical way. Instead we are developing a more sensory narrative in which your subconscious consumer desires are fulfilled instantaneously and to this end we are trialling different decades in history. Can you please all ensure your emote headsets are plugged into the portal on the side panel of your suit.'

Several attendants walked among us and checked that headsets were connected to the portals and in the exact probing position. I noticed that my portal was numbered eight; I wondered if that had any significance given that there were ten of us.

'Feel free to walk round the park, sit by the lake, and sunbathe in our ozone free environment.' The preppy girl continued, 'If you desire anything, simply think it. Our virtual android factory will pick up your requests and will deliver it to you instantly. As this is market research, we will only deliver requests to be consumed in the park. But obviously we intend to roll this out universally should it work; I mean prove successful. Enjoy your afternoon ladies.'

'It's so beautiful here I wish I had a camera...' Kimberley replied wistfully. Before she could finish her sentence a Miyake multifocal camera was gently dropped in her lap by a sparrow like drone.

'I bet that's expensive,' I replied impressed.

Kimberley and I gambolled over to stripy deck chairs overlooking the lake and two bottles of crisp Icelandic water appeared.

'Did you ask for water?' Kimberley asked.

'No, but I thought about it.'

We were distracted by several high-pitched consumer wish fulfilment shrieks as a group of young woman emoted entire ranges of cartoon couture, bling bling and Coachella and the sky was now full of drones delivering leopard print puffer jackets with condom shaped buttons, gold plated clip-on Yorkshire terrier earrings and stoned teddy bear iPhone cases emblazoned with Disney characters.

'Did you hear about Daniel Huffington's new start up?' Kimberley asked as we adjusted to the postmodern simulacrum of Seurat's impressionist painting now three dimensionally layered with the very best of lewk couture.

I wasn't entirely sure how to answer? I had seen it on Facebook and didn't want it now.

'It's called attack dogs and cannabis,' she continued playfully.

'I know,' I said pointing at the headset.

'He's used a synergy algorithm. If you run products associated with drug dealers through google marketing, the most likely associated high profit yield products are attack dogs.' She replied with a playful 'let the mayhem begin' glint to her eyes.

I deliberately tried to think of nothing.

Kimberley continued, 'So he decided to set up a hybrid business that combines the two.'

I winced, 'Kimberley, can we stop talking about this. I really don't want either dropped in my lap.'

Kimberley chuckled mischievously, 'I wonder what happens if you request big items.'

'Please don't say, size of an elephant,' I said and then clasped my hands over my mouth. 'Kimberley I'm not finding this relaxing at all. Do you think you can turn it off?'

'Probably not, they're trying to work out how many consumer products we desire in two hours.'

I sighed anxiously and a voice in my ear said, 'Would you like some cholinesterase inhibitors.'

I must have emoted unease at this suggestion because a small bottle of CBD was slowly lowered with a note that said, 'Take three drops.'

Kimberley suggested we walk down to the lake and we stretched out on inflatable pink flamingos in the pretend sun and watched as other more daredevil members of the research group jumped into the not real water lake in tulle explosion prom dresses. Kimberley thought of a picnic hamper and I tried to relax but was still very aware of not thinking too much, if at all.

'How's the corset connection going?' Kimberley whispered.

'Not sure really, I went to Patlib and found my grandmother's patent but I can't claim any retrospective copyright infringements because, well, it's all been left too late.'

A GOV.UK patent application form fell from the sky.

'Lucky it wasn't a dead billionaire.' Kimberley laughed.

'But I still think Bill stole the corset design from my grandmother and I would like to find out why she kept quiet about it, even now.'

'Family honour, far more rewarding than money,' Kimberley nodded and ducked as a Scottish kilt was dropped by her side.

'Are you Scottish?' I queried.

'Maybe.'

'What did you find out?' I said ducking as Best Girl's latest William Morris clothing range dropped down.

Kimberley shrugged, 'One of my old gentlemen used to be a Saville row tailor and got some referrals from Daps, said he saw Solley Weitzman at a rodeo in New Jersey in 1957.'

'Really, what like on a horse?'

Kimberley hooted, 'No actually he was a stall owner, my gentleman wasn't sure what he was selling but whatever it was, they were going like hotcakes. The cowboys couldn't get enough of them.'

'Was the rodeo called Cowtown?' I asked remembering the matchbox I had found.

'Yes, how did you know?' Kimberley replied impressed.

'I found a matchbox in Dora Duffy's head.'

'And people think I do weird things.'

'It was a mannequin Dora Duffy,' I explained.

'That's okay then,' she replied deadpan.

I tried not to think about anything.

'My old gentleman gave me a photograph of himself dressed as a cowboy, if you want to see it.' Kimberley squeezed her eyes shut.

'What are you doing?'

'I left the photograph in the locker so I was trying to emote it here.'

'Would that be teleportation?'

'Anyway, I asked him if he thought Solley Weitzman became Bill Wonder, and he was very sure they are the same person.'

'Just like Oswald Finlay said.'

'Who's Oswald Finlay?' Kimberley said as a deflated helium balloon landed at her feet.

'I met him at Bill's funeral, he used to work at Dapplewhites, remember your Mr Dapps knew him.'

'Oh yes, that was book day, wasn't it?'

'Maybe, you were dressed as a raunchy Alice and Mr Daps was the white rabbit mashed up with the Mad Hatter.'

'Just the white rabbit, the other part is his actual persona.'

'A red queen costume is about to appear, isn't it?' I said as costumes for all the characters mounted up around us.

'I hope so.'

'Kimberley is Miyake industries sponsoring this event?'

'Yes, one of the richest men in the world is funding our shopping expedition?'

'If this is a shopping expedition,' I sighed as I watched simulacrum swans glide over the fake lake. 'You know Miyake turned up at the British library looking for the Silver corset patent.'

'Really, whilst you were there looking for the patent,' gasped Kimberley, 'Ooo how very cloak and dagger.'

'No, before that.'

'How do you know that?'

'Time loop.'

'Really?'

'No, I made friends with the patent researcher, well she made friends with me and she told me. Fortunately, she hates the evil Wonder Empire.'

'They do say you need to be careful to make friends on the way up because you wouldn't make them on the way down.'

'Literally, in Bill's case.'

'I wonder if you can make friends whilst falling off a balcony,' Kimberley mused.

'I'm more interested in Miyake's MO. I wonder if he knows about the book.'

I must have dozed off as a shadowy Bill dressed in a pink corset and bowler hat was chasing me across London rooftops, whilst discordant music played like a pounding irregular heartbeat. As I leap from one rooftop to another, I slip, but stop myself falling by holding onto a metal railing with one hand; the shrill music is becoming louder; then someone reaches out a hand for me. I smile gleefully as Bill spirals down through an endless repetition of office buildings. Then in a female oedipal trajectory, the scene starts all over again. Then a high-pitched alarm woke me from my somnolence.

As I came to, Kimberley was shouting, 'Sadie, Sadie wake up. We're not allowed to sleep with the emote headsets on.'

I opened my eyes and discovered the whole range of Amanda's Secrets lingerie dating back to about 2010 stacked around me, several chainsaws and a ladder.

'I'm not even going to ask what you have been dreaming about,' she sighed.

A loudspeaker echoed through the artificial park informing us that we had five minutes left and as the distant edges of the park had started to dissipate, I hurriedly packed up. 'Come on, Kimberley,' I edged nervously.

We went back to the changing rooms and were asked to remove the computer chip in our portals.

'Oh you're number eight,' one of the attendees said with a smirk as I handed him my computer chip.

'Kimberley, when you signed my consent form for me, what did you sign away.'

'Oh, something about artificial intelligence gathering and digital avatars.'

'Like recording and potentially marketing our thoughts sort of stuff.'

'Yes I think so, how exciting is that Sadie, just think your thought patterns today could be used in an AI of tomorrow.'

I didn't find this exciting at all.

On the tube, I noticed a new fashion paradigm. Lots of people were wearing Bashion boiler suits. I listened in on a conversation between a Bashion adapter and her yet to be converted friend, 'It's great, it doesn't need washing. It changes colour to suit your mood. You can carry everything you need in it. It even has protein shakes and medical supplies and a tent and a built-in funnel potty. I don't think I will wear anything else ever again.'

'What, even when it's not fashionable?' asked her friend.

I looked down the carriage and noticed that half of the commuters were dressed in a Bashion, men and women. Although aware of the code of tube travel, (never speak to anyone unless it's the last tube home and everyone is pissed), I was too interested in where the Bashion boiler suits had come from to care. 'I'm sorry to bother you, but where did you acquire your Bashion suit?' I asked her politely.

After an initial frosty stare, the girl answered me, 'It was delivered to me, courtesy of Miyake industries.'

'Did you order it or pay for it or anything?' I asked surprised.

'No it just arrived in a parcel with a note that said "wear me", with compliments of Miyake industries.'

How can that be, I thought, the epistemology of fashion doesn't cater for durable long-lasting freebies. 'Did you have to sign something, offer your first born or a kidney in exchange?' I asked.

'No,' the Bashion fellow passenger replied sharpish, whilst giving me a stalker alert look and she turned to her friend and said, 'Come on Lisa we're getting off now.'

Chapter 18
Subcultures

School was not fun on Monday; the teachers all seemed scared and paranoid in a 1984 way. They also looked smaller and non-descriptive now they were all dressed in Bashion boiler suits. Mags Twill did look slimmer and less stained though.

'The whole gang back together, well almost,' I said cheerily as we arranged ourselves in the staffroom for the Monday morning meeting

'We are not allowed to engage in unscheduled conversations anymore,' Alice whispered.

'Really… wow,' I began but quickly realised why I needed to be quiet when Sharleen bad-arsed her way through the staffroom door and everyone stood up and saluted.

Sharleen appraised us all with her spindly evil eyes.

'Right, let's begin. The good news is profits are up. The lickety-split courses are doing well, well done Maggie Twill.'

'The what?' I whispered to Alice.

'No talking,' Sharleen hissed whilst prodding me with a Lolita parasol.

'Introducing a maintenance and cleaning element to the course was, if I do say so myself, a stroke of genius on my part and now all auxiliary services at the school are staffed and managed by fee-paying students. But I'm concerned about the margin on the 12-week courses. My objectives for the next few months are to have all courses producing an 87% profit. To achieve this, there will be another round of redundancies. This time it will be teachers. Oh and Sadie, Lickety-split is my joke name for the six-week course, because it's so short and so profitable. It's hilarious, isn't it?'

Everyone laughed nervously.

After the meeting, everyone else nervously scurried off and I felt rather underutilised. I attempted to teach some students about the economic, social and political factors that lead to Christian Dior's New Look in 1947. I even put an image of a model wearing the full skirt, wispy waist and soft shoulders on a whiteboard in a classroom full of students licking envelopes.

'So why do you think the French government, church and industrialist that made textiles, were so interested in a fashion trend?' I asked, but no one looked up.

Harvey Jones did politely say, 'Sorry Sadie, we are all too busy getting these invoices out. If we don't, the Wonder bank will increase our interest repayments.'

So I went back to the staffroom. I was flicking through a wedding dress catalogue circa 1981 trying to solve one of the biggest mysteries of the eighties. How did they fit Lady Di and her large puff sleeves, full meringue and 8 metre taffeta and lace train into the tiny glass coach?

When I heard lots of ingenuous high pitched, 'Hello how are you and you look wonderful,' emanating from the staffroom door. As nobody usually bothers to pretend to be nice, I was intrigued.

There were four new arrivals in the staffroom, a fast food assistant, a merman, Rod Taylor (the actor from the 1960s film, "The Time Machine" based on the HG Wells' book) and Polly Rootbeer.

Polly Rootbeer was talking to Alice, 'Yes, I've just started work on a new project that explores body positive advocacy and transparency in our new wormhole reality.'

'Ohh that sounds fantastic, what's it called?' simpered Alice ingratiatingly.

'It's such a multi-layered digital platform piece that I haven't quite found the right words to embrace it with, but my last work entitled "12 years a whore", went for over a million at Sotheby's.'

The fast food assistant was, I think, Bill's daughter Candy, who is or was a very famous Haul girl. Candy looked like a chutzpah-loaded Sharleen type of girl, who must have been Bill's favourite. She was one of the early, now very famous, self-created celebrity Haul girls and would regularly have 10 million viewers on her site called Candy Lovechild. Her original concept was seemingly straightforward; she would arrive on camera, giddy with excitement and eager to show all her buys from her busy shopping spree in London that day. No one questioned why the clothes were always from Wonder shops, because it was obvious that Wonder always had the best fashion. She would take the clothes out of the bag as if exposing some ancient lost artefact for the first time in centuries and her eyes would ignite with consumer gratification. She spoke in a mildly erotic, posh totty, innuendo, naïve way and would often rub the garments suggestively across her breasts and lips a bit like Nigella.

If it was a really good haul she would salivate and a tiny bubble of spittle would appear at the side of her mouth. When she started hauling, no one realised she was Bill Wonder's daughter and her titillating discourses were deemed as genuine, "keeping it real", grassroots flogs. The posts were extraordinarily successful promotional vehicles for Wonder clothes and statistically resulted in more sales traffic than the TV programme where people who can't sing but desire celebrity, go and make fools of themselves.

Her cover was blown a year ago by an undercover journalist posing as a fan who had shop-stalked Candy on several swag sprees. Candy of course wasn't going out and buying clothes; she was attending corporate marketing meetings at Bill's headquarters and would leave with two or three bags of swag. She had been accused of astroturfing, of strategically constructing the posts and deceiving her viewers, which was true. She was then blamed for a series of swag haul thefts. Hundreds of genuinely poor fashionistas had stolen from mid-range fashion shops and had been caught when they posted their booty online. In their defence, they claimed that the 'Candy Love Child' videos had driven them to steal to feed their hyper consumerism addictions, which Candy Love Child had groomed into them from a very young age.

In a controversial move, the eminent High Court judge Anthony Buccaneer agreed with the defendants and in his summing up said, 'I don't agree with the insidious deluding of the general public by virtue signalling. I have no other choice but to reduce the thieving swaggers' sentences to community service and counselling.' Candy Love Child was so unnerved, she had a full 17-minute blog breakdown and heartily apologised for her astroturfing. She had pulled her hair back, wore no makeup and cultivated some very large spots on her chin, so everyone decided that she must have been genuine. I'm not sure whether we have forgiven her now or not.

Polly Rootbeer was eyeing Candy up and said in a snarky way, 'I see you're wearing the latest Eldorado, part of the chauvinistic purr-suits range.'

Candy nodded in a dismissive "what if" way.

Polly mocked, 'You must be high on Chauvinistic purr-suits, you look like you have brought the whole autumn/winter collection, including the "portion of chips" phone cover and the burger shaped handbag. It's interesting you can pull off fast food, red and yellow, most people can't.'

Candy glared at her.

Polly continued, 'It's kinda strange don't you think, that the fast food chain immediately changed its uniforms to khaki and brown. It was as if they didn't want to be associated with a high-end fashion company.'

Candy sighed and Polly Rootbeer turned to the Rod Taylor look-alike.

'I love your retro – operative, Isambard Kingdom Brunel outfit bro.'

'Thanks, have you seen my headphones designed to look like an old pocket watch?' he replied excitedly as he took the headphones out of a battered leather doctor's bag.

'Have you got a time machine too,' Polly laughed.

The Rod Taylor look-alike looked confused and a bit deflated.

'To go and save the girl from the troglodytes,' Polly replied with a shrug.

The Rod Taylor look-alike still looked blank.

'Don't worry about it,' Polly said, turning to the Seapunk.

'I guess it's okay to belong to a clearly identifiable trend if you're being ironic,' she said ruffling the Seapunk's aqua blue green hair.

'And oh, look at your cute little shoes, are they wrapped in designer pretend seaweed,' Polly gasped in a mock cutesy way.

'But,' Polly continued in a mock dramatic way, 'where are the barnacles, you simply must have barnacles darling.'

'You're such a bitch, Polly,' Candy said, 'leave the twins alone.'

The twins, I was now guessing, must be Bill's sons who hadn't joined the family business and were rumoured to be, well, a bit thick.

Polly ignored Candy and continued, 'Did you see my friend Miranda Eclipse's UK Oceanic tour. It was seminal because it was the first time Seapunk's subculture heritage moved from internet joke to real world happening.'

The Seapunk looked confused.

'You do know your outfit started as an internet joke in 2011, with an overshare from the iPhone of a famous New York DJ (who is of course a very good friend of mine).'

The Seapunk shook his head cretinously.

'OMG, you're not being ironic are you,' Polly gasped.

I was now beginning to wonder what Polly Rootbeer, who was clearly a sophisticated early adopter, was doing hanging out with these second, maybe third generation followers. Although I guess it made a lot of commercial sense if Bill paid top dollar for a subcultural cool monger like Polly, to hang with the family. Bill's teenage customers were desperate to believe in a just-beyond-their-reach well of untapped coolness, and Polly Rootbeer really was the new perennial teenager, trailing a scent of cool wherever she went.

'What does your T-shirt say Polly?' asked the Seapunk somewhat earnestly.

'It says what happens when the algorithms take over,' Polly replied nonchalantly.

The twins looked at their phones.

Polly had just started to say something when Mags Twill blustered in and said, 'Oh heavens, so sorry about your dad.'

I blenched when it dawned on me that Polly Rootbeer must be Bill's oldest child – the one "no one ever heard about." If this were true, then Polly Rootbeer wasn't some kid from a trailer park in some aspirational lacking Midwest American town, population 179. Her mother hadn't worked in the diner and fed her on deep fried burgers, her father was not an alcoholic who shot through when her mother's heroin habit got too much. Polly Rootbeer was actually the wealthy privileged daughter of a billionaire. I always thought being poor and angst made for subcultural cool that was the point. It was the one thing money can't buy. Now I realised she must be all marketing hype too.

'Thanks. As I was saying, I've just launched my new multi-platform digital, actual reality fashion masterpiece called Bashion,' Rootbeer said.

'That sounds interesting,' Mags Twill replied in a bemused way.

'Bashion is a non-deteriorating, self-cleaning and apocalypse appropriate onesie. Once you have bought it, you will never need to buy another item of clothing ever again,' she replied proudly.

'Erm, how would that work commercially?' Mags Twill hesitantly asked.

'Wow, that sounds really useful,' said the twins.

'Yes, it is. The Israeli scientist who designed it has installed several life extending gadgets.'

'Like what, like does it have a toilet?' asked the twins.

'Yes. It includes a portable toilet hose which recycles urine into drinkable water if required,' replied Rootbeer.

Candy huffed and gave Mags Twill a here we go again look.

'And a mini medical hospital which includes an emergency plastic, laser surgery kit,' chirped Polly.

'Does it have a tent?' asked the twins.

'Yes, and a protective cloaking device.'

'Where can I buy one?' asked the twins, mobiles at the ready.

'How fashionable,' Candy sneered, 'or is it really the ultimate teenage rebellion, are you fucking over the family business because daddy didn't buy you a pony?'

'Well actually he did buy me a pony, well stables ...' Polly fired back but stopped mid-sentence as Maggie Cotton ambled in.

Polly looked astonished and gulped, 'What are you doing here?'

Maggie Cotton replied, 'I work here.'

'I know who she is, she's Agent Gingham from Bag Rags,' Candy interjected excitedly.

Polly screamed at Candy, 'And how do you know she's Agent Gingham. You little cow, you've been going through my notes again, haven't you?'

Candy snorted, 'Notes? What, you mean your scribbles that you send away and pay someone else to turn into digital real-world art campaigns.'

I could sense the twins physically commune, 'They're at it again,' and they sat down and played on their phones.

'Agent Gingham,' gasped Mags Twill, 'the commie-terrorist one, who plastered giant photographs of Wonder's best-selling red chequered dress, with hand drawn breasts and penis on them all over the shops on Oxford Street in the seventies?'

'I was young,' Maggie Cotton added looking abashed.

'Agent Gingham who's married to Alfie Poor, the spoken-word poet and anti-capitalist revolutionary, now serving a life sentence in prison for the failed bombing of Bill's flagship shop on Oxford street,' continued a confounded Mags Twill.

Maggie Cotton indignantly replied, her ditzy Blondie veneer clearly disguising the heart of a revolutionary, 'It was hardly a bomb, it was filled with ribbons and would never have hurt anyone but because of pressure from retail giants, mainly your father,' she added, accusingly pointing at Polly, 'the judge dished out a life sentence.'

Candy suddenly screeched at someone standing outside the glass petition.

'Sharleen, Sharleen, wait I'll come to you,' she cooed as she fled the room.

Mags Twill, Maggie Cotton and Polly Rootbeer stood awkwardly staring at each other.

The Seapunk and the steampunk were twin-communing I think – as one or the other would answer non-spoken questions.

'Yes.'

'Shopping, I expect.'

'Missing Dad.'

Then Candy burst back into the staffroom looking stricken; her hair extensions matted into her panda mascara sodden face.

'What's wrong Candy?' the twins asked as they led her to a chair. 'Yes,' they added soothingly. 'No, it doesn't make sense, one minute he was here the next gone.'

Candy didn't say anything; she was crying too much. Poor Candy, she really did seem upset about her father. Cool Polly asked in an exasperated way, 'What's wrong with her now.'

The twins stopped pacifying and said in unison, 'Dad died.'

'Yes, I do know. I'm not that up my own arse,' replied Polly.

The twins both raised an eyebrow and psychically emoted 'really.'

Maggie Cotton, I noticed, had retreated sharpish.

Then Candy wailed, 'It's gone, it's all gone.'

'What's gone?' asked Polly.

'The money,' sobbed Candy.

'What money?' asked the twins?

'Dad's money,' Candy snorted.

'What?' the others exclaimed in disbelief.

Rootbeer grabbed Candy by the collar and pulled her close and hollered, 'What exactly do you mean?'

'I was talking to Sharleen about my new shoe range and Dad's solicitor rang and said there's a problem with Dad's will.'

'We better go to the solicitor's office now,' Polly said assertively and the fast food shop assistant, the Seapunk and the Rod Taylor lookalike tottered after her.

The staffroom emptied and as all the students were now gainfully employed running the school and parts of the Wonder Empire, I decided it was an opportune time to do some sneaking around the third floor.

I had just reached mannequin Dora Duffy when I heard a crashing sound followed by someone saying, 'Oh shit, I've broken it.'

'Can I help?' I said poking my head round the door to Bill's office. My sudden appearance led to even more frantic gasps of fear as two students, who had clearly never cleaned anything before, knocked over a bucket of soapy water and crashed a mop into the abstract painting that hung above Bill's desk. The glass covering the work cracked and the contents slid down the wall.

'No,' wailed one of the students.

'Oh double shit,' said the other, 'You have just destroyed Bill's Anai Foucaitt. I bet it's worth a fortune as well.'

'Anai Foucaitt, the conceptual artist,' I exclaimed.

'Yes.'

'Do you know the work?'

'Well no, but she was my grandmother's best friend.'

Both students sniggered.

'You mean he was,' one said.

'No, she,' I replied,

'Everyone knows she was really a he.'

'Do they?' I replied confused.

'Have you been to the retrospective at the Tate, it's very good? He was brilliant really, the way he pointed out the illusion of everyday reality.'

'Yes, but I never really got the obsession with New York taxis though.'

'I know right. And like why all those photographs of weedy looking men?'

'What? You mean you didn't get that? It's about how you don't need to be good-looking or attractive to be photographed.'

'Really?' I said, feeling blindsided by this new revelation, whilst also becoming transfixed by the contents of the Anai Foucaitt that were now sliding down the wall behind Bill's desk. Anai's abstract conceptual work had formed into a solid mass and now that I finally had a chance to look at it at close quarters, under the full glare of the fluorescent lighting strip and without its glass cover, it was a washed out pinkie grey colour with black lines. And the black lines defined its shape. And its shape was very definitely corset shaped. There was also a label with five silhouettes of tailors' mannequin dolls in varying improbable shapes with the name "Bobena Silver, London" embroidered in Bloomsbury script sticking out of the lining.

'Girls, why don't you go and find something to dry this mess up with. There are some toilets down the hall and I'll see what I can do to make good' I said, very keen to get them out of the office.

As soon as the students left, I picked up the sodden mess and plopped it in my fake designer Hermes shark bag. I replaced the sodden corset with the Mila Schon, which I fully submerged in the mop bucket and then wrung out. As I was sellotaping the Schon into a sort of corset shape, I caught sight of a wispy shadowy creature darting down the corridor.

'Wait,' I shouted

The sprite-like character stopped and nervously turned round.

'I know who you are and what you have done,' it said nervously hopping from one ballerina lace sparkle stockinged toe, to the other.

'Oh okay, but I don't want to hurt you,' I said soothingly.

The creature suddenly darted up close to me and peered at me with her disconcertedly wide weak eyes. 'Are you good or are you bad,' it muttered nervously, 'Now the very fabric of capitalist society is unravelling so quickly, I can no longer tell.'

She was wearing a mustard yellow and orange knitted circle dress which was several sizes too big and she smelled of pencils and wee. To try and calm her anxiety and hopefully create a sisterly bond, I did what women always do and said, 'I love what you are wearing. Did you get the Zandra Rhodes from the walk-in wardrobe?'

'Yes,' said the strange feral creature.

'It's great in there, isn't it,' I continued, trying to build a relationship with her. She nodded enthusiastically.

'Have you been through the shoe section?'

'Yes,' she nodded.

'Which ones do you like best? I think I like the Giuseppe Zanottis glam rock glitter zip punk, or maybe the Timmy Toe silver and black stiletto.'

'I guess my all-time favourite has to be the 1938 Ferragoma platform shoe,' she replied enthusiastically.

'Good choice, good choice, the high heel suggests the anti-gravitational effect of a dancer en pointe. Whereas the platform announces an earthbound weightiness more like the flat steps of modern dance.'

We both nodded lost in shoe bliss.

'I'm Spooks,' she said holding out a grubby hand.

'Spooks,' I said reluctantly shaking it. 'Spooks, Jonathon's student?'

'Yes. What's dripping from your bag?'

'Nothing.'

'Are you stealing something again? You know bad things happen when you take things away from here.'

'What do you mean?'

'I know you took the book.'

'Bill's photograph album, how?'

'I was watching you. What's so important about it?'

'Have you been watching me the whole time?'

'Yes.'

'Did you like my corset?' Spooks asked earnestly.

'The Rumpelstiltskin one?'

Spooks sort of jumped up and down in an affirmative way.

'I didn't steal it you know. I accidentally put it in my bag when the lights went out.'

'Bill went mad when he realised it had gone. He spent the whole night rampaging around the school. He ran around screaming that his fortune was lost and I think he cried in his office, that or he was having some sort of stroke.'

'There's nothing much in it. Just several photographs of men's chests and torsos.'

'Sounds like the photographs at the Anai Foucaitt retrospective, you should go and see it, you know.'

'Yes I will. I wonder why Bill panicked so much when he found out the book was gone.'

'He said they are bound to kill me now that the book is lost.'

'Really, did he mention any names?'

'He said something like Treadmore, maybe Treadwell.'

'Treadwell,' I repeated feeling a little faint, 'could that elderly psychopath still be on the loose?'

Spooks looked confused but interested, 'Oh, he did leave a note on his desk. I took it. Thought I could add it to an art piece but it didn't fit in. Do you want it?' she said, taking out a heavily folded piece of paper.

I greedily opened it out and read, 'Tell Bobena she has won.'

'Won what?' I said looking at Spooks for clarification.

'Won whatever they were competing about I guess,' Spooks replied sagely. 'I have to go now and make today's body part installation. Think I will base it on shoes, mountains of shoes. Bye, see you next time,' she said as she pattered away.

Chapter 19
Gussets

I phoned Judith Trouser, she sounded like she was in a wind tunnel, 'Sadie, Sadie. Sadie, is that you?'

'Can I come over? I have something to show you. Are you at home? Do you have a home?'

'Just come to the office.'

Judith Trouser was pacing around her office when I arrived.

'Sadie, have you noticed how everyone is wearing Bashion boiler suits nowadays?'

'Yes,' I said stepping back.

'Oh, you have one too,' she said, eyeing me suspiciously.

'It's compulsory now at the Fashion school.'

Judith sort of patted me down, 'Do you think it links up to something, like a higher being, or a control centre?'

'I don't know. Miyake industries, the big Japanese pharmaceutical company, are producing them.'

Judith replied nervously, 'Do you think they are deciding who to give them to, based on ethnicity or race or something?'

'Maybe age,' I nodded. 'I have only seen people under forty wearing them.'

'Like Logan Runs.'

'I think that was thirty,' I replied accidentally pressing the air pollution purifier.

Judith breathed in gratefully. 'So to corsets,' she said, 'let us fiddle whilst Rome is burning.'

'Absolutely,' I agreed

I emptied the sodden material out of my shark bag and watched it flop about like a fortune telling fish. When it stopped wiggling, Judith peered at it.

Judith started to salivate. 'Is that what I think it is?' she said, her lips quivering with desire.

I said nothing but teased it out a little more and watched as her eyes went all dewy and then said, 'Yes.'

Judith snatched the girdle up and pressed it to her bosom and wept.

Eventually she composed herself enough to say, 'Sorry, I have waited so long to see one in the flesh, it's the holy grail of 1950s foundational undergarments. Can I keep it? '.

'Sorry no, I only borrowed it, it will have to go back from whence it came before someone notices and I get sacked again.'

'Why have you brought it?' she said despairingly.

'I need your expert advice.'

She sighed wistfully.

'This is a copy of the original patent,' I said unfolding my photocopy, 'and this I'm pretty sure is the genuine article, would you say they are technically the same?'

Judith put on her spectacles and peered studiously at the girdle. 'Well, beam me up Scotty. Yes, I would say it's the same design as your grandmother's corset design but are you aware of this?'

I shrugged.

'Look at how the hip area is padded.'

'OK.'

'And there is no cleavage; instead the pectoral region is flat and slightly raised.'

I nodded again.

'And the oblique area is sculptured into six tight, inflexible, muscle regions,' she said looking at me intently.

'Okay.'

'And Sadie, there is of course this,' she said holding up the triangular shaped girdle and pointing to the gusset.

'It looks like a codpiece,' I gasped.

Judith nodded.

'Judith,' I asked. 'Why would you design a girdle with a codpiece, slightly raised pectoral regions and a sculptured oblique area, using a material that maintains a solid shape rather than holds it in?'

Judith shrugged knowingly.

'Bill Wonder wasn't making girdles for women, was he?'

Judith shook her head.

'He was making them for men.'

'The marketplace must have been flooded with undergarments for women but who was making girdles for men? No one I suspect.'

'But, men gave up looking pretty in the 20th century,' I replied confused

'And before that it was all about ostentatious display,' Judith replied whilst stretching out the girdle.

'Like the 17th century Peacock with his tight doublets with slashes to expose flesh.'

'And highly decorative gold-laced waistcoat,' Judith said whilst nodding in agreement.

'Intricately laced whisk collar and elaborate high heel shoes.'

'Red-soled high heels if you were a king.' Judith added.

'And the 19th century dandy with his Titus hairstyle, Beaver top hat, fob watch and tasselled hessians.'

'But if the Wonder girdle was designed for men, not women it's like one of the biggest fashion history secrets out there.' I gasped.

'I know it's as if men displaced their own bodily narcissisms and pleasure in beautiful well-made clothes onto women and then instead of becoming unburdened, became riddled with body image insecurities that they wouldn't talk about because it would have been considered effeminate,' Judith replied.

'Of course this was why you couldn't find a Wonder girdle for love nor money. We were asking the wrong people.

The wrong gender. We should have asked the grandfathers not the grandmothers.'

I thought about the ruminations of this gender twist, 'And so all those adverts, celebrity endorsements and even the Naked Corset film, they weren't aimed at women, they were aimed at men.'

'Yes, I guess so,' agreed Judith. 'It explains the end bit when Angel sends the male solicitor the corset in the post.'

'I thought that was an act of female liberation.'

'I guess not. It was actually far less obscure.'

I felt a bit strange thinking about the possibility that I had misread thousands of adverts and marketing propaganda for so long, what else had I been viewing from the wrong side?

Identity, performativity, objectification?

'Are you okay, Sadie?' asked Judith, 'You look a bit spun out.'

'I feel a bit strange,' I agreed.

'What are you going to do next?' asked Judith, sounding a little concerned.

'Apart from a profound reappraisal of the great masculine renunciation, I still don't know how this is connected to my grandmother, and whether this explains why Bill died. So I think I need to try and get some sense out of my grandmother.'

'If it helps, I would say that as the fundamental design of the corset with the nine segments is the same as the patent, so it probably would count as a copyright infringement.'

'Thank you, I think it does a little.'

'Why don't you take a break from all this today? I find it always helps to do something different if you're stuck on something. Have you been to the Anai Foucaitt at the Tate? It's very of its day, but I hear the works are now selling for a fortune.'

'I didn't even know there was a Foucaitt exhibition until this morning.'

'It's a pop-up exhibition; new works have just been uncovered. It seems like a really big deal; they even moved the Picasso New lover's exhibition to make room for it.'

'That's unheard of, isn't it?'

'Well, it is being sponsored by Miyake Industries.'

'I guess money still talks.'

'It is very good. It's called Exposed and the artist has included lots of never seen before pieces. You know technically if the work is new, it's not a retrospective, the Tate seems to have forgotten that.'

'You know Anai and my grandmother were childhood friends. They grew up in the same tenement in the East End. I think she helped her out at the Silver workshop; at least I have a photograph of them there.'

'Did you know her as a he or she?'

'I always thought she. I still have a photograph of Bubbe and Anai going to New York on the QE2,' I said carefully not mentioning the other photographs.

'What, you mean part of the pastrami on rye series?'

'I guess so; Bubbe said they were going on a business trip to Lackeys. And Anai needed a sandwich for part of her installation.'

'Lackeys, you mean the large American chain store that specialised in lingerie. If your grandmother had a successful meeting with them, it would have meant a massive order. I'm guessing in the thousands. Do you know the year they went?'

'April 1957, it's written on the back of the photograph.'

'Just before the Wonder Girdle was launched.'

'Yes.'

Millennium Bridge was packed full of people waiting to get into the Foucaitt exhibition. As I jostled my way through the Bashion clad crowd, a large dirty swan or possibly goose glocked something like, 'Is that you?' The bird then held out a human hand and I offered it a pound in the hope it would move away.

'Sadie, its Tanya,' the bird said indignantly.

'Tanya.' I gasped, 'what has happened to you.'

'I'm in between jobs at the moment,' she said looking crestfallen.

'I'm going to the Anai Foucaitt; would you like to join me?' I asked hoping she would say no.

'Yes, please,' she glocked, 'but, ermm can you pay?'

'Sadie isn't this fabulous,' Tanya said as we entered the first exhibition.

We travelled through a tunnel of hazy light and giant female images dressed in fifties designer outfits revealed themselves and then occluded.

'I love what they wore back then,' Tanya said, pointing to two enormous holographic feet.

I nodded, 'the black ones are scalloped Babydolls, about 1950.'

'What about the yellow and leopard flatties.'

'I think they're Capezio.'

'Are they standing next to a yellow New York taxi cab?' Tanya asked

'Yes and that one wearing a fitted lilac wool twinset and black beret.'

'Look at the next one,' Tanya glocked pointing at the next holographic image which appeared and disappeared depending on where you stood.' I think they look like the same ladies but are they arguing about something. And I think they're standing outside Lackeys, the New York department store. It's so cleverly incongruous isn't it?'

I nodded whilst nervously skirting from one giant hologram to the next.

'The small one looks like Audrey Hepburn, and the other bigger one looks like Marilyn Monroe. The small one looks very angry. I knew this was coming.' Tanya chortled excitedly.

The next hologram in the series was of the Audrey Hepburn look-alike, sucker punching the other lady in the face.

'I'm not sure why, but she definitely deserved that,' Tanya smiled enthusiastically. 'And now look. Are they on the ground brawling?'

I nodded again as I segued from one giant hologram to the next trying to stitch it all together.

'Sadie, Is the blonde one wearing a Balenciaga sack dress?'

'Yes, it's a Balenciaga sack dress.' I replied.

'Has it ridden right up?'

'Yes. That type of unstructured style will do that if you're brawling. 'I said feeling like I had fallen into 'The Looking Glass'.

'And here's a taxi driver trying to separate them, and his lanyard looks like it's caught in the zipper of her underwear.'

Tanya honked uncontrollably as the final hologram revealed itself. The Balenciaga lady was lying on the pavement. Legs akimbo. Her corset now straddling her ankles. The focal point was the Balenciaga ladies gusset and interestingly we the audience were now privy to one of Anai Foucaitt's famous often huge penises.

'Sadie it's called, "Never in the history of fashion has so little material been raised so high to reveal so much that needs to be covered so badly" that's brilliant, that's a Cecil Beaton quote you know. Do you think Foucaitt is making a statement about cross dressing and restrictive laws about wearing "the dress of the opposite sex"? I think we were just as bad in Britain. It was called "the Labouchere amendment of the Criminal Law act 1885". It was known as the blackmailers' charter, because it allowed judges and lawyers to prosecute virtually any behaviour (loosely termed as homosexual) for gross indecency. I think Oscar Wilde and Alan Turing were convicted under it. Sadie, are you okay? You have gone awfully quiet. Do you need a coffee?'

'I'm not sure if I'm looking at art or reality,' I muttered.

'What do you mean?' Tanya asked puzzled.

'I really don't know,' I replied searching the room for some potential clue.

'Is that a young Miyake Hayat?' Tanya said, pointing excitedly at an alabaster head to torso statue of a slim Asian man, with a pectus deformity. 'Oooh I met him you know; oh I guess you probably did. He is so well-mannered. Do you remember last year's "End of year awards day"? Bill had invited his billionaire club Carlo Monte Carlo was there I guess it must have been before Bill punched him. Oh look there's a photograph of him on the wall over there.'

I turned and looked at a blown up photograph of a chubby amicable young man.

'Oh look, Sadie, there's a photograph of Alex Wedge, the lead singer of the Lost Ways, he was always my heartthrob.'

Alex Wedge was clearly many people's heart throb as his photographic image was creating quite a stir and lots of Bashion boiler suits had turned bright pink.

'Is that the president of Lithuania?' Tanya asked, craning her neck on an inquisitive angle, whilst pointing to a very weedy young man, 'They have just made a Christmas calendar of him doing macho things.'

'That one is John Green, USA head of international procurements,' Tanya glocked excitedly.

'Has he got a pigeon chest in that photograph? He always looks like a big burly man when you see him at the UN conferences.'

'Yes, I think it is,' I said appreciating how the exhibition screens had been designed to look like the sleeves of an old photograph album

'That barrel-chested man is Fritz Haber, head of the EU.'

'This part of the exhibition is called "Little man, big man". Why do you think there are serial numbers under the photographs? They look a bit like concentration camp photographs? Do you think that's the point, like is Anai saying anyone could have ended up in a concentration camp even men who went on to be very successful world players, although I don't think all of them are successful, but maybe it's just because I don't recognise them all,' Tanya glocked away happily. 'Do you recognise anyone else Sadie.'

I was having trouble trying to differentiate reality, art and a photograph album I had accidentally taken from the fashion school then lost at my grandmother's nursing home. And I think my sense of perspective was unravelling. I left Tanya in the coffee shop regaling fellow exhibition goers about her life with Miyake and took the train to Bournemouth. This time I was determined to get the complete story out of Bubbe.

Chapter 20
Shapeshifters

When I got to the nursing home, Bubbe was awake and looking decidedly compos mentis, I would even say chipper as she happily regaled other old ladies with name-dropping stories about her life in London.

'Sadie, that's good timing,' she said waving me in, 'Everyone meet my granddaughter Sadie, she's a murderer you know.'

'Oh how lovely. I'm Iris, who did you kill?' asked the lady sitting next to Bubbe.

'Yes, hello, and I didn't kill anyone,' I replied shaking her hand.

My grandmother nodded in a 'she did you know' way and then said, 'Oy vey, I'm not sure about that nasty shade of green your Bashion boiler suit has just turned though.'

'I don't really like you telling people that I killed Bill Wonder,' I remonstrated.

'You killed Bill Wonder,' gasped Iris.

'Wonder, she killed Wonder,' Laughed another resident. 'Well, he had that coming for a long time, well done dear.'

'Yes, bravo to the young lady,' added another resident.

'Bubbe, can we go to your room? I have a few things I want to talk to you about,' I asked amongst the clatter of congratulations.

'I was just telling my,' Bubbe stopped and added contemptuously, '"friends" about Hayat Miyake, the richest man in the world. And Sadie two visits in one week, what, am I going to die?'

'Do you know Hayat Miyake?' I asked amazed once again with my grandmother's ability to throw a curveball

'What. Of course I do. I designed his first corset. Sadie, his success is all down to me.' Bubbe said pointing at herself and smiling proudly.

'Why did he need a corset Bubbe?'

'You think they're gonna promote a man with a squashy chest, erm what do ya call it,' she said holding her hands in an inverted V shape.

'Pectus deformity,' I offered.

'Yes that's it squashy chest. No confidence, what you gonna do.'

'I think they do a rather horrible operation nowadays and push a metal bar under your ribs.'

Bubbe growled, 'Sadie, you make them a padded corset and they become the CEO of the most profitable company in the world. So you see his success is down to my…' Bubbe paused and looked at me.

'Corsetiere skills.'

Bubbe nodded proudly.

'But wait, Bubbe, are you saying that you made corsets for men.'

'What, you think your clumsy Bill Wonder managed to do it on his own. Bill couldn't make corsets. Your Bill couldn't make tea. Yes Sadie, all those men crying out for discreet corsets that made them look more like mensch, whether it made them behave better, I think not. But I certainly gave them a shapeshift.' She laughed gutturally.

'So you made corsets for men at Dapplewhites then.'

'We had to work, how do you say, clandestinely. In the fifties, men were considered faygel if they worried about their appearance so we used Dapplewhites as an overcoat.'

'Front,' I offered.

'Bill was fat and could never shift that stomach of his so I can see how he came up with the idea,' Bubbe said, tightening her fists and gritting her teeth. 'Yes, women's wear, come buy your women's wear, pantyhose, stocking but really it was all a fabrication, what we were really doing was making foundational undergarments for men.'

'Then what happened.'

'Lackeys,' she growled.

'What happened at Lackeys?'

'Lackeys heard about our little operation and offered us a deal. A very lucrative deal.'

'That's great.'

'Great, great, I can't deal with your mishegoss anymore,' she said whilst indicating that I should leave.

'But wait Bubbe, I have something to show you if you just answer a few more questions.'

'Okay, as it's you, Sadie, what do you want to know?'

'What was wrong with the Lackeys' deal?'

'Oh vey, she doesn't understand, my granddaughter still doesn't understand. The idea was to mass produce the corsets and well call them girdles.'

'Okay.'

'Bill was all for it, it will make us very rich,' she said. I said I don't want to make cheap schmutter gggirdles with standardised sizing so they would never fit properly. I could never have allowed that to happen to the Silver corset.'

'Bubbe, why did you let Bill take all the credit for the Wonder girdle? I mean you designed it; he really was the marketing man.'

'What take credit for that nebekh verkmanship he was spewing out of his factory? You are a real crazy if you think I would have done that.'

Bubbe started to look thunderous again, 'You know Sadie, it's not always about the money, sometimes when people make things they are proud of, they want to maintain the quality and craftsmanship.'

'You mean like producing corsets that fit, rather than girdles that don't.'

'Yes.'

'So Bill didn't threaten you or trick you.'

Bubbe breathed out like an indignant horse, 'Of course he didn't threaten me, that bubula, that schmendrik. I didn't like that he sold the corset out, but I was never scared of him.'

'But you ran away to Devon, you were hiding there.'

'Hiding in Devon, have you ever tried to hide in Devon, everyone talks to each other, everyone knows everyone else, no it's easier to hide in London, no one wants to know in London.'

'But why did you leave Dapplewhites.'

'Err you know, Sadie, it was the end of the fifties. Corsets were out. By 1965 no one was even wearing knickers. Everything comes to an end, particularly in fashion.'

'But I spoke to Mr Dapplewhite; the younger, he said you just disappeared one day.'

'Arr that boychick, how is he?'

'He's old now Bubbe, but seems well, sends his regards, said you used to scare him as a boy.'

'I used to pinch his checks, make them red, yes it would have hurt, but that's good for boys,' Bubbe laughed. 'But I guess I did have to leave rather quickly after the incident but I didn't want to get tied into another ten-year franchise at Dapplewhites; I saw the writing was on the wall. See Sadie I always know so it worked out well.'

'What incident?' I pressed.

'What Sadie, I am getting tired now.'

'I know Bubbe, just tell me about the incident at Dapplewhites and I will give you your present, you will like it.'

'The incident at Dapplewhites,' Bubbe repeated looking hazy.

'Please Bubbe,' I replied, willing her to stay cognisant for a few more minutes.

'Yes, oy vey all this talk about a misunderstanding, what was I doing yes, I remember I was making a corset for Mr Dapplewhite and I needed to work out his dimensions and I'm not sure why, maybe because he was the boss, or just an English man, he wouldn't let me measure his petseleh so I was using your Bill as my mannequin and I was just rough

183

hemming the gusset when that mashugana Treadwell walked in. He went crazy, called Bill a pansy, puff, abomination. Bill said, but it's for Mr Dapplewhite but then he went real crazy.'

'So Bill was thrown out of Dapplewhites because he was wearing a corset, did you get into trouble for, well, looking like you were.' I had to stop.

'Treadwell didn't seem to mind what I was doing, but the stories about it got out and I felt a bit like a shiksa. Another reason for me to skedaddle. Always leave at the mountain peak. Bill wasn't happy about me leaving though'

'And he went off to America and signed the Lackeys deal.'

'Yes and made those horrible nistkasten girdles and I moved to Devon. The end. Where is my present?'

I handed Bubbe the corset from Bill's office, neatly wrapped in tissue paper. Bubbe's eyes shone with excitement as she opened it. ' Sadie, is it really the corset I was making for Mr Dapplewhite, look it is, see the registration number on the label they all relate to the numbers in the book, see 1405, it's Mr Dapplewhite's, you can see how the gusset has only been roughly stitched. You clever, clever girl.'

'Oh yes Bubbe, where is that book,' I asked.

Bubbe looked blankly at me.

'Bubbe I've just come from the Anai Foucaitt exhibition.'

'It's very good isn't it? That's why we needed the book.'

'Who's we.' I asked nervously.

'Sadie, Hayat and I.' Bubbe replied, eying me as if I was an idiot.

I tried to process everything Bubbe had said, 'is this to do with the fight you had with Anai outside Lackey's?'

'Of course it's to do with the fight. We had just been having this conversation, don't you remember? And they say I have early onset dementia; I think you better have the test. Never mind the quality, feel the width, basic principles of fast fashion. Please tell me you remember,' Bubbe replied looking concerned

'But we were just talking about Bill Wonder weren't we?'

'Oy vey, I will tell you the story again but this is the last time. So put down your phone and listen with your ears.'

I did what I was told.

'Anai helped me build the business, the corsets for men,' she replied slowly.

'Not Bill or even Solley?'

'Bill was Anai, you klutz, why don't you understand that.'

'What?' I said feeling chintzy.

'Sadie, are you okay? Your Bashion has gone white.'

'Bill was Anai,' I repeated.

'Yes, of course he was. Bill wanted to become an artist but his mother said no, no you go work in the schmutter trade like the rest of your family. So Bill and I came up with his alter ego Anai Foucaitt. Oh boy, oh boy she was a clever one, one of the first female conceptual artists in the UK you know. We used my cutaways to make well stuffed shmoks. The British public loved them and I don't think she would have made such a name for herself if she was plain old Solley. But his mother was right; there was no money in conceptual art in the fifties, not like now, now you fill a plastic head with blood and it's geshmak.'

'So why were you fighting outside Lackeys.'

'We were fighting over the book.'

'Why?'

'The book listed all our clients, of course, over a thousand. You think Lackeys would have signed a million dollar deal based on puffy air. No, you see Sadie, my client book proved the numbers, proved the demand. And I knocked him right out. He went down and his dress goes up.' She chortled and patted the muscle in her arm.

'Yes you must have a good right hook.' I agreed.

Bubbe beamed.

'Bubbe have you been looking for the book all this time.'

'Well yes and no. I didn't care. I moved on. That's what you say nowadays isn't it?'

'But.' Bubbe said, leaning in and whispering. 'There's lots of important men, very important proud vain men like Hayat that didn't want the information in that book coming out, corsets, weak chests, fat stomachs. Not what men wanted uncovered. Not in my day. Now I'm not so sure. Men wearing girdles in the fifties, sixties, seventies, maybe okay in the eighties. Boy oh boy' She giggled gaily.

'So do you think Bill was using your client book like a burn book?'

'I love that film Sadie. We watched it downstairs last week. Regina George is my favourite. You should be more like her. You might be successful. But yes I think Bill was using it as a burn book.'

'So Hayat Miyake was after the client book.'

'Yes, and the rest Sadie and the rest. But then what do you know out of nowhere my granddaughter sweeps in. Sweeps in, steals the book and kills Bill.

'I didn't kill Bill.'

Bubbe nodded proudly. 'Hayat said his men had finally located it, just about to get it. He said they should only kill Bill if they had to. But you, you showed no mercy. Straight in. Straight over. No mercy. That showed real chutzpah. Hayat said his men were very impressed with my chubby little English granddaughter.'

'Thanks, I think.'

'You know Sadie, Bill and I had a wager about who would make the most money before they died. Bill's get rich quick fast fashion narish or my quality craftsmanship based on true artist endeavours which of course included all works created by Anai Foucaitt.'

'And I guess Bill won.'

'Did he Sadie, did he? It didn't help that you killed him but fortunately my old friend Hayat helped me out. Said if I get the book, he will sponsor an exhibition of Anai's works. He said it was about time he stopped having body image issues. He said the time was right to stop hiding behind insecurities.'

'But Bubbe, Bill was like a billionaire. An exhibition at the Tate isn't going to make the same amount.'

'Sadie I am not gantseh, although the merchandising from the Anai Foucaitt exhibition is selling like boy oh boy. No, when I asked for Hayat's help I told him about my Bashion boiler design.'

My Bashion boiler suit suddenly turned a deep brocaded gold 'You own Bashion!'

Bubbe nodded triumphantly. 'Well 49 percent, Miyake Industries has the controlling share, always a good businessman Hayat.'

'You own 49% of Bashion, you know everyone in London is wearing one now.'

'London, London, everything happens first in London, but has it reached Devon yet.'

'I have no idea, but I think one of your care assistants was wearing one, does Bournemouth count.'

'Was that Joel, he's such a nice boy.'

'Did Polly Rootbeer have anything to do with it?'

'We used her for the line-on marketing, I don't understand any of it but she has 12 million followers. Is she a religious nut or mashugana cult leader?'

'Bubbe, did you steal the photograph album from me that day when you had me thrown out for being a bit tipsy.'

'A bit tipsy, you were shickered. But I had to steal it. After you killed Bill, it threw our plans out and we weren't sure whether we had actually enough time left for the general public to notice that cheap, poorly made clothes aren't actually worth buying.'

'I didn't kill him,' I said indignantly.

'Okay bubula, you stole the photograph album as well as not killing Bill. But then I said to Hayat, let's use some of the photographs in the book in the exhibition. I said, enough of the body image issues. It's time to come out of the closet with the corsets. We also managed to pick up twenty major investors who said body issues, what body issues?'

'That's brilliant Bubbe. I said pressing the music for special occasions button on my suit. Nothing happened.

Bubbe looked a little concerned and said 'And so Sadie, my plan is for Bashion to take over the world. I'm already thinking about upgrades. But one thing Sadie I will tell you, no one else, as you killed Bill before we had fully tested the Bashion boiler suit there may be some glitches.'

'Don't worry I don't really mind if the music button doesn't work, I can just use the built-in headphones.' I reassured her.

'And Sadie I have plans for you too. No granddaughter of mine works for other people. I need to take my pills now as I have a business conference in a few hours so come back again but leave it for a few days.'

'Yes, Bubbe.'

I picked up a newspaper for the train journey home. The headline read, 'Creditors seek to wind up the Wonder Fashion chain after huge financial irregularities are discovered. The dissolution of the retail chain will commence immediately as the accountancy firm LQNH believe the company is in debt to the tune of £685 million. The financial expert Tim Lucky has explained that the Wonder fast fashion paradigm has been losing momentum for several years now and the extraordinary success of Miyake Industries Bashion boiler suit has added to their woes.'

I think the man sitting opposite was rather surprised by my exuberant high five.

When I got home, Kimberley was waiting for me; she was wearing a Bashion but had made some provocative rips so that quite a lot of her cleavage and upper thigh was exposed.

'Sadie, Sadie, guess who I bumped into at Dapplewhites by the "The perfect weave for material happiness" wall.'

I shrugged.

'He's tall, blond hair, taught me visual design at the fashion school.'

'From your semiotic clues I think I'll have to say Jonathon.'

'Yup.'

'They released him?'

'He said Trixie came forward.'

'How, she was at the Pepto riot. I bumped into her on the square just after Bill died.' I replied.

'What you were there, I thought you had been suspended.'

I jerked my head nervously and then with glib ability said,' Oh yes, you're right I saw Trixie on the news report.'

Kimberley narrowed her eyes 'Anyways it wasn't Trixie Jonathon saw it was her friend Susie. Trixie had asked her to cover her classes. I guess you can't just ask someone to cover your lesson without telling anyone. Guess that's why they didn't come forward sooner.'

'How is he?' I asked.

'I'm not sure Sadie, he's changed. I was wearing a chest hair swim suit and see through plastic trousers over, I think, supermarket jeans.'

I frowned trying to make sense of it all.

'He looked nervous and not like a cultural intermediary at all.'

'That doesn't sound good.'

'Have you heard about the Wonder Empire; it's going down quicker than barmaids' knickers? I love that expression; it's so marvellously sexist and offensive.' Kimberley giggled.

'Yes, I was just reading about it. Sounds like it's been going tits up for years. Maybe my grandmother wasn't spot on with her timing this time.'

'What?'

'I went to see my grandmother. Did you know that Anai Foucaitt was really Bill Wonder?'

'What no way. Anai Foucaitt is like the coolest person to come out of the fifties. Why did Bill choose to become a fat cat capitalist rather than her?'

'Yes, it was an oddly unfashionable choice,' I agreed.

'Did your grandmother design the Wonder girdle then?'

'Yes,'

'But there's more to it than that.' Kimberley said, narrowing her eyes again.

'You know how we could never find a Wonder girdle and when you did track one down its proportions were all out.'

'Yup'

'The Wonder girdle wasn't a woman's girdle, it was designed for men.'

'But it was the seminal undergarment of the fifties. Every woman had one.'

'Maybe every woman bought one but they were designed for men.'

'It could be argued that the corset never really disappeared: it just changed into new types of foundation garments.'

'What.'

'It's a quote from one of your lectures. Why did they pretend it was a women's girdle?'

'I guess men weren't ready to admit that they wore body enhancing clothes. It was the fifties and men had far more important things to do than worry about body image. That was the women's realm.'

'Hey 'was the photograph album some sort of burn book. Did Bill use it to blackmail billionaires?'

'My grandmother wasn't sure; she did say that Hayat Miyake didn't want anyone to know he wore a corset, so yes it had that potential. My grandmother also said I should be more like Regina George.'

'No I'm like Regina George.'

'Yes I guess you are.'

'I bet Tom Strip wouldn't want people to know he wore a corset or Ken Huddle.'

'That is true.'

'What did your grandmother and Bill, or whatever name he went by fall out over.'

'That was ideological rather than gender based. My grandmother wanted to continue making high quality made to measure corsets. Bill was happy to sell out and mass produce standardised girdles. My grandmother refused but Bill took the design to Lackeys and signed some massive sell out deal anyway.'

'Your grandmother was right, fast fashion is so last century darling. So that's why she punched him outside Lackey's.' Kimberley laughed.

'Well, yes, I guess it's reached the rejection stage of the fashion cycle. You've been to the Anai Foucaitt at the Tate.'

'Everyone has been to the Anai Foucaitt.'

'You know my grandmother collaborated with Anai on all her artworks. They came up with the whole concept together.'

'Well blow me, maybe she's the coolest thing to come out of the fifties.'

'She also owns 49% of Bashion now. She designed that for Miyake industries. ' I said, pointing to Kimberley's flirty pink boiler suit.

'Guess she's really rich now.'

'Maybe but for her it was always more about intrinsic value.'

Kimberley added in a Yoda-like way, 'I will never wear anything other than a Bashion boiler suit again.' And it turned a noble midnight blue.

'But I see you have already started to accessorise it. That's where fashion starts you know.'

'What are you going to do now? Have you lost your job again?'

'I think I have, my grandmother said she has other plans for me.'

'What, like making corsets?'

'Unlikely she always thought I was a klutz. I don't think I have the manual dexterity to make corsets.'

'I'm thinking of changing careers myself. Prostitution is so one dimensional '

'What about information gathering, you're very good at that.'

'Yes I am and actually I have already gathered a lot of interesting data.' Kimberley said in an ominous way.

I nodded uneasily.

'Do you fancy a drink? I know a great place called the Chemist Laboratory; they mix cocktails with dry ice, they're really expensive.' Kimberley asked.

'I was going to say let me get changed but no one cares anymore'. I said putting the Bashion boiler suit into day time drinking mode.

'Sadie, did you ever find out who killed Bill?'

'No, although my grandmother is convinced I did.'

'And did you?'

'No,' I replied indignantly.

Kimberley looked thoughtful and said, 'Does it matter?'

'I'm not sure. Although I guess there are loads of people who would like to know how the story ends.'

The Epilogue

How to Kill a Billionaire

The next day I checked my Bashion boiler suit for any mind control apparatus and as I couldn't see anything obvious, I decided to accessorise. I added a Rosie the riveter neckerchief, rolled up the sleeves and then for good luck, added a dash of Chanel perfume as, to quote the lady herself, 'A woman who doesn't wear perfume has no future,' and today I felt like I had.

The school was closed and a large insolvency notice was taped to the door. I took the stairs up to the third floor for the last time.

As I walked past mannequin Betty Boop, she started her smutty chant, 'He couldn't take my boop-oop-a-doop away.' I looked at her and she stopped but when I started walking again, she said, 'Koko will save me.' I gave her a Jonathon icy glare as I entered the walk-in wardrobe. I walked through the shoe collection which would no doubt be sold off soon and once again appreciated how well Bill had curated it. The collection started with a Joseph Box shoe of 1890, with its iconic teapot shape and juicy red ribbons. Then a 1958 Roger Vivier purple and azure blue high heel for Dior sent a wave of Pepto frenzy down my spine. Next to them and still in their original box was a pair of Mary Quant ankle boots with a daisy motif on the sole, so that the whimsical wearer could leave a daisy motif in rain puddles. I cuddled a Louboutin 2008 and salivated over the rock and roll cobblers' collection. Then I spotted my holy grail of shoes, a pair of 1938 Salvatore Ferragoma platforms. They beckoned with their seductive gold, kidskin and layered cork caked red, purple, orange, gold, white and green rainbow skin. Their allure was too strong for me to resist and as I picked one up, I saw a small card inside which read, 'My dear Judy I hope you like them, I designed them for you. S.' I felt like weeping with joy, I had found my shoe nirvana. I put the Ferragoma on and twirled and danced and somehow my feet were no longer my own, they belonged to the shoes. I felt like the peasant girl in the fairy tale who insists she has a pair of shoes fit for a princess only to discover they are enchanted and continue to dance, night and day, rain or shine, through fields and meadows, and through brambles and briers. I was only able to take them off because I saw a pair of 1970s white platform shoes with a Bianca Jagger backstage pass and the moment of indecision somehow broke the all-consuming spell that had taken hold of me.

I wrapped the Ferragoma in a Theo Porter kaftan and put them in my 2007 IT bag for the fashion-conscious woman, with its ironic postmodern eco-conscious slogan, "I'm not a plastic bag" and then I continued to walk on through the belly of the wardrobe running my hands through the entire original BIBA collection, down some Dior's, past a tuxedo suit on through fake fur coats and the real fur coats, and the luxury pyjamas.

I stopped at the Burkin 55. Some people think that 49 is the complete set and that's because they don't know or realise there is one more Burkin. A Burkin so rare and expensive that only people with untold wealth (or penniless dreamers who teach fashion history) have heard of it. The last Burkin went beyond monetary worth; it was called the Himalayan Burkin and was encrusted with rare diamonds and made out of albino crocodile skin. I held the bag up and stared in wonder as the light bounced off the diamonds and then I put it in my IT bag as well. I reasoned that as I was now unemployed and my pension had probably disappeared, I was owed some sort of severance pay.

I made a conscious decision to leave the wardrobe after that as something was happening to me that wasn't quite in my control and I sensed I needed to stop before it went too far.

As I pulled the door shut on the wardrobe for the last time, a small creature dressed in Versace 1990s "That dress" bobbed up in front of me and said, 'Sadie, I have been trying to speak to you.'

'Spooks,' I gasped, shaking myself out of materialism.

'Sadie, you look a bit possessed.'

'Yes, I feel quite different,' I replied.

Spooks was shivering and looked bedraggled in the dress that was several sizes too big for her. 'Have you heard about the Wonder Empire?' she said anxiously hopping from foot to another.

'Yes, it's gone into receivership, the school and all the shops have closed down, I think 20,000 people have lost their jobs overnight.'

Spooks looked desperate and very hungry.

'Do you fancy a cuppa and a bacon sandwich?' I asked.

She nodded heartily, 'Yes please, but I've no idea where we can get one round here.'

'Yes, sushi doesn't really cut it,' I agreed.

We said our goodbyes to mannequin Dora Duffy and the other corsetieres and closed the door on the Fashion school and walked into Soho and did find a retro, modern cereal bar which reluctantly agreed to make us bacon butties as long as we didn't sit in the window.

'So,' I finally asked, 'what did you want to speak to me about?'

'Well,' she began tentatively, 'I know what happened to Bill and I guessed you would want to know too, what with you being there and partly responsible and all.'

'Was I partly responsible? I still don't actually know what happened to Bill?'

Spooks slowed down into an almost Zen-like calm and I became slightly concerned she was going into food-eating shock. Finally she rather surprisingly asked, 'Have you read Passage to India?'

'What, that book by Forster?' I answered.

She nodded, 'You know the part when they ask who attacked Adele, and some wise old mystic says, no one attacked her, everyone attacked her.'

'Yes,' I said.

'Well,' said Spooks even more slowly.

'Well what, who did it?' I exasperatedly asked.

'Ermm,' Spooks said wanly.

'Are you being so slow and hesitant because you think I killed Bill, is that it?' I queried.

'Well that's my point. I think you did, I did, and we all did.'

I groaned and thought my grandmother would probably say something like, 'Are all young people so overloaded with information they can't decipher a discernible narrative thread anymore?'

'What does that mean? Are you saying Bill was some sort of directionless victim, a person that the fate or misfortune or really bad luck happens upon in some, well Passage to India imperialist culturally misunderstood way?'

'Sadie, I think you should calm down, your boiler suit is turning red.'

I looked down; she was right. Until this point it had been a reassuring navy, now it was crimson.

'Okay,' I sculled as the boiler suit turned to a more calming purple.

'Does it control your impulse urges as well?' asked Spooks, suddenly very interested. 'I was thinking about the Pepto riots and I know Carlo Monte Carlo was trying to be the first to create an urge impulse response to certain clothes. I have a friend who was an early adapter Bashion wearer and she's completely changed now.'

'Really, how?'

'Well, she keeps going a bit abstract and talks about buying high-end clothes that she really can't afford as if it's her divine right to dress in Moschino. Do you think you should just take the Bashion boiler suit off, you know before it starts doing things to you?'

'I think it tried earlier, I was in Tanya's walk-in wardrobe and well I felt a sort of uncontrollable bloodlust for the clothes. I only just managed to get out.'

'Yes, I saw you flapping away,' Spooks nodded knowingly. 'You know it's Bill's walk-in wardrobe not Tanya's, don't you?'

'No I didn't, but guess it explains the slightly less trashy aesthetics.'

We both nodded.

'Why did you steal the old corset that was framed in Bill's office?'

'Well it was actually my grandmother who designed it.'

'Oh is that why you killed him? I thought Miyake Industries paid you.'

'I thought we all killed him.'

'Well I do hold myself partly responsible. But you were definitely the straw that broke the camel's back, that's a funny saying, isn't it?'

'Yes, it is. But Spooks, can you just finally explain, what does "we are all responsible for killing Bill" discourse actually mean?'

'Yes, okay,' replied Spooks, 'shall I start at the beginning?'

'Yes as long as the beginning's not a come full fashion cycle sort of thing.'

'So,' began Spooks as she cleared her throat, 'this is what happened or at least the chain of events as I saw it.'

I settled down to pinkie grey.

'I was on the balcony making a present for Jonathon. He's been very kind and let me sleep in the mannequin cupboard. I have moved up to the ninth floor, now it's empty.'

'Yes, I heard about Jonathon letting you sleep there,' I nodded.

'I was making him a mannequin Karl Marx as a special treat. Jonathon called our class the lumpenproletariat, so I was sure he would love it. I spent weeks finding the perfect Marx's coat. Which is very hard nowadays because clothes are not made to last. But that coat allowed him entry to the British library and that had to be special.'

'You mean the coat that Marxists use as a metaphor for commodity fetishism, to represent the inequalities between

199

the rich and poor? In a time when the poor literally had to pawn the shirts off their backs to buy food,' I added, wondering where Spooks would find such a mantle nowadays.

'Yes,' agreed Spooks. 'And indeed Marx's materialism can quite easily be linked to questions about cloth material, so a truly fitting epitaph to the suffering of the poor today as well as in the Victorian times.'

'Did you find a worthy simulacrum,' I asked intrigued.

'Well not exactly, I made one myself out of industrial strength bin bags.'

'Actually that's brilliant,' I agreed, impressed with her resourcefulness, 'and obviously you are aware of the bin bags' significance in punk's anti-materialist rhetoric.'

'But of course, that's why I chose it,' she smiled.

'Do you think Jonathon would have got the significance?' I asked doubtfully as I suspected Jonathon's response would be more like 'what designer label is it?'

'Well I don't know because I never got the chance to give it to him.'

'Yes right, other things did rather supersede that.'

'So, as I said, I was happily adding the finishing touches to my Marx mannequin and I was singing revolutionary songs, well more like ditties about shops and clothes and the concept of capitalism and the exchange value of a coat in Victorian times. Then I stood mannequin Karl Marx up to put on his heavy overcoat and he looked so snug I couldn't help but shout out, "You couldn't buy Marx's coat in one of your crappy fast fashion shops Bill Wonder." Then as if by magic, Bill lurched onto the balcony.'

'Why was he lurching?'

'He was toppling around in those high stilettos he insists on wearing when he thinks no one is around and he was muttering about his missing photograph album, saying, "Now it's gone, disappeared, I'm in trouble. She will win."'

'Oh yes, you told me that last time and I guess he'd been up all night looking for the photograph album, which isn't a good thing to do when you're his age.'

'He was so wrapped up in his problems, he didn't really notice me or Karl Marx. Then he froze and looked absolutely terrified and said, "Bobena Silver, not Bobena Silver, not you. Couldn't they have sent anyone but Bobena Silver?"'

'Bobena Silver is my grandmother, I'm pretty sure she wasn't on the balcony and besides, she's like 94.'

'He was gesturing to the window that is right next to your desk and there was a woman with a Chanel bob and 1950s Chanel wool suit pointing angrily at him.'

'But that was me. When I got suspended, I went and got a new look, actually I think Gita suggested it.'

'Well I recognised it was you with a do over but Bill didn't. He was really panicking and kept repeating, "She's back, back from the dead. She's after her corset and she's going to kill me."'

'Actually, she isn't dead yet.'

'Okay but he was wobbling around like crazy. Then he relaxed a little and said, "I will write her a cheque that will get rid of her." He leaned on the balcony railing to balance whilst he wrote it and then must have spotted mannequin Karl Marx glaring at him. He looked so scared; I almost felt a little sorry for him.'

'A ghost of his past sins on one side and the leading exponent of anti-capitalism on the other,' I added ponderously.

'Then,' Spooks continued, 'something like a mini earthquake took hold of the building and he dropped his cheque book over the balcony. At that same moment, he leapt up to try and retrieve the cheque book, a small Miyake drone bashed into his head and the trouser hem of his cheap polyester suit got caught in his stilettos and Bill just catapulted clean over the balcony.'

I was too stunned to speak for a stitch. Was this a terrible accident or the fitting end to a tyrannical mega manic billionaire? Spooks was right, it wasn't who killed Bill it was what; guilt, the supernatural, idealist views, socialism, the underground, cheap clothes and ridiculously high stilettos.

'Old-fashioned concepts woven into a postmodernist narrative,' I said, 'how very fitting.'

'I collected the cheque he was writing; it landed by the bins, you know where you were hiding.' Spooks handed me the crumpled cheque. It was written out to Bobena Silver but that was as far as it went.

'Did you say she was your grandmother?'

'Yes, she made the corset that was the prototype for the Wonder girdle.'

'That's why you kept creeping around the school after getting suspended?'

'Yes.'

'Oh one more thing, I met Mr Miyake on the stairs as I ran away. He gave me his card, asked if you and I were free to do another job for him as we did such a neat job on this one. He said it was executed beautifully and he really liked how we made it look like an untidy accident, or as he said, there is simply no way of proving it either way.'